MURDER FORETOLD

Agent John Bentick is not enjoying his latest assignment for British Intelligence — personal bodyguard to Nargan, an abrasive foreign diplomat on a covert mission to exchange military secrets. On their arrival at the isolated house of Professor Dale in Cornwall, Bentick senses an atmosphere of mystery and menace generated by Dale's latest invention — a sinister machine that is somehow shaping the destiny of everyone in the house. Soon he finds himself a helpless pawn in a figurative chess game that can only end in death . . .

Books by Denis Hughes
in the Linford Mystery Library:

DEATH WARRIORS
FURY DRIVES BY NIGHT
DEATH DIMENSION
BLUE PERIL

DENIS HUGHES

◆

MURDER FORETOLD

Complete and Unabridged

LINFORD
Leicester

First published in Great Britain

First Linford Edition
published 2017

A catalogue record for this book is available
from the British Library.

ISBN 978–1–4448–3382–9

Published by
F. A. Thorpe (Publishing)
Anstey, Leicestershire

Set by Words & Graphics Ltd.
Anstey, Leicestershire
Printed and bound in Great Britain by
T. J. International Ltd., Padstow, Cornwall

This book is printed on acid-free paper

1

Distasteful Assignment

The man at the desk, who looked up abruptly as John Bentick opened the door, was grey-haired, with deep lines channelling the sides of his mouth as if there were a bitter taste inside it. His forehead was broad and smooth beneath its covering of iron-coloured hair, and below that, his eyes were piercing and almost black in tone. Those eyes were the only really human-looking feature about him. He sat there staring at the newcomer thoughtfully for a moment, elbows on the edge of the desk, legs sticking straight out. Then he smiled, and when he did so something happened to make him a human being instead of the hardened master under which Bentick and men like him worked loyally.

'Ah, Bentick,' he said. 'I sent for you. Sit down.'

Bentick frowned slightly, then relaxed in a deep leather chair that faced the desk. The agent was just under thirty years old; he found a zest in life that amazed his friends and won admiration among them. He was of middle height, brown-haired and boyish-looking, with a sharp-featured angular face that was always ready to crease into laughter. There was little enough humour in the work he did, but somehow he found opportunity even in that. Being a secret agent on Cain's hardened staff was exacting work, but to Bentick the good of his country was always at the fore. He was ready for any assignment that Cain handed over.

Cain said: 'I sent for you because there's a tricky little job to be done, and I think you're the best man to handle it.' He stopped as Bentick opened his mouth. 'No, don't say anything until you've heard the details. I very much doubt if they'll appeal to you, but that can't be helped I'm afraid.' He paused, fixing the younger man with a stare that was shrewd and penetrating, yet friendly for all its granite qualities.

'You know the present state of tension under which this country is living, of course. It's a state in which at any moment war could break out, unless certain things are handled with the greatest delicacy. One of those things is the secret of the latest armour-destroying projectile our scientists have devised. If it can be used in the right way, it'll be a powerful tool for maintaining the peace. But if someone puts a foot wrong, there's going to be trouble on the most colossal scale that civilisation has ever known.'

Bentick crossed his legs and nodded. 'I've heard things myself,' he admitted. He knew of Britain's latest development of atomic weapons, and could easily foresee the devastation that another war would cause. 'Is anyone likely to put a foot wrong?'

Cain nodded thoughtfully. 'That's what we have to prevent at all costs. And that's where you come in, Bentick. You're not going to like this job.'

The other grinned. 'Depends on what it is,' he said.

Cain put his fingertips together and gazed through the window behind Bentick's head. 'Tomorrow a visitor comes to Britain. He's one of the leaders of a powerful nation that's an ally of ours. No one, I may add, is fond of the nation, but the fact is that without its alliance we would not be in a very strong position if trouble came. You follow?'

Bentick nodded slowly. He knew which nation Cain meant. It was powerful, no doubt about it; and situated as it was in the most strategic position in Europe, its friendship was vital to Britain. Yet everyone who knew more than a smattering about international affairs was distrustful of the necessary alliance. It had been forced on them by circumstance, not from choice.

'Go on,' said Bentick quietly. 'What's our visitor coming here for? Negotiations?'

'In a manner of speaking, yes,' replied Cain. 'He'll be bringing details of a development in scientific warfare which he's agreed to exchange for a modified plan of the armour-piercing projectile I mentioned. The exchange will be carried out with the greatest secrecy possible.'

'And I take it that I'm to be the watchdog for the meeting? Is that it?' Bentick

4

wrinkled his nose in a grimace of displeasure. 'What's the name of our visitor?'

'Nargan. You've heard of him, haven't you?'

Bentick's lips went tight. Yes, he'd heard of Nargan all right! The most unpleasant man that politics on an international scale had ever produced. And it looked as if he, Bentick, was to be responsible for the safety of the diplomat during his stay. An unwanted assignment, he thought. However, when Cain issued an order, it was carried out without argument. He had that effect on his men, and they stuck with him through any kind of trouble that fate could devise.

'You know,' said Bentick soberly, 'I hate the notion of Nargan getting away with any of our secrets, even if he gives us something we haven't got ourselves in exchange. I wouldn't trust him as far as I could throw him!'

'Which wouldn't be very far!' said Cain with one of his rare smiles. 'They tell me he's putting on weight.'

Bentick grunted. He foresaw a thoroughly distasteful period ahead of him.

'Let me have the details,' he said. 'I might as well know the worst.'

'Nargan arrives by air tomorrow morning. You're to meet him and escort him to a destination I'll give you later on. He'll be travelling in disguise, and there's no one else in on the visit except you and I and the person who arranged it after careful consultation with the cabinet. The utmost secrecy has been maintained, so that although a limited number of people know what's in the wind, no one but us knows exactly when and where the meeting will occur. Is that clear?'

'Perfectly,' answered Bentick. 'Even the Special Branch aren't in on the visit?'

'No. That's how it's been arranged.' Cain broke off with a frown. 'It throws the entire responsibility on us,' he added grimly. 'Frankly I don't like it any more than you do, Bentick, but that's the way it is. This man whom we distrust, yet are compelled to trust by circumstances, is coming to England and must be guarded. Nothing, you understand, must happen to him. If it did, then I think you can guess what dire results would ensue. Any harm that comes to Nargan would fall on the head of this country, and with international affairs in their present state of tension it could only mean appalling calamity. Do I make myself plain?'

'You certainly do, sir!' answered Bentick. 'I won't let you down, but I can't pretend to fancy the job.'

Cain eyed him narrowly. 'It isn't for us to like or dislike the work we do,' he said quietly. 'All I'm hoping is that nothing happens; then you'll have no greater worry than putting up with a very unsavoury customer.'

Bentick raised a rueful smile. 'All right,' he said. 'Now let me have the full details, and I'll be ready to take over the moment Nargan arrives in the morning.'

Cain gave a satisfied nod. Then: 'Have you ever heard of Professor Dale?'

Bentick pricked his ears up. Where did Dale come in? Aloud he said: 'You mean the noted scientist? The man who's been experimenting with cosmic radiation for the past five years? Yes, of course I've heard of him.'

'Professor Dale is the man behind most

of the advance work on the atomic projectile. He's a little eccentric, naturally, but he's a clever man to have working for Britain in times like this. The brain in his head has been even more priceless to mankind. Without it, I feel sure we would've had another war on our hands before now.'

'Agreed. What about him?'

'Nargan's meeting our own representative at Dale's house in Cornwall. You'll be responsible for seeing that he gets there safely and carries through with his consultation. Professor Dale's place is ideal for the meeting, since only he and his ward are there. It's a lonely spot, and a very old building. Dale has his own laboratory there, and from what I hear he's engaged on some fantastic work of his own.' He smiled again, thinly. 'If you're lucky, you might discover what it is; but I warn you that Dale's a very queer customer, so don't go snooping around uninvited!'

Bentick gave a shaky laugh. 'It's most unlikely! I'll be sticking as close as glue to Nargan all the time. Don't worry about that, sir!'

Cain nodded. 'I know I can trust you, Bentick. The plane from Europe arrives just after dawn. You'll have a car at your disposal at the airport, and Nargan will give you a pass to establish his identity. No one will know who he is or what his business involves. You'll take him straight to Professor Dale's house. Dale has told me that a separate suite will be available for Nargan during the time he's there. That's all I can tell you now. Any further instructions will be handed to you before you leave for the airport at dawn.'

Bentick rose to his feet and stood looking down at Cain. His youthful face belied the grimness that lurked in the back of his mind. This assignment, if all went well, would merely be an irksome part of his duty, but if anything did go wrong it would be the finish of his career; he knew that from Cain's expression and the manner in which the man had spoken. And Bentick's career as an agent of Britain was as precious as life itself.

'Very good, sir,' he said. 'You can leave it to me. When does our own man arrive at Dale's place?'

'Noon the day after tomorrow,' answered Cain. 'He'll be leaving again in the evening.'

Bentick nodded. 'I'll report when the job's done.'

2

Nargan

Bentick was a very thoughtful man as he left Cain's office and made his way back to his own apartment. Cain's brief description of the situation had intrigued him enormously, as well as what he had said about the mysterious Professor Dale and the products of his mind. Dale was certainly a useful man, he reflected, and his Cornish home would be an ideal meeting place for the coming vital rendezvous between Nargan and the person representing Britain in the important exchange of information. Bentick had never met or seen Nargan, but his reputation was an ugly one that travelled ahead of him wherever he went. The man was gross and as hard as granite. Bentick could see that this job would definitely be an unpleasant one.

The remainder of the day passed

uneventfully. News of the international situation was noncommittal, but to those who had access to inside information it was grave. The nations of the world were tottering on the brink of another holocaust that would surely see the end of sanity on earth. Only by the most careful handling could the position be steadied. Part of that steadying action — a major part of it — rested with Nargan. And his safety was Bentick's responsibility. Any slight leakage of the truth behind the coming secret meeting would be fatal, for jealous nations would seize on the exchange of information as being a step towards war instead of away from its peril. Bentick felt the weight that rested on his shoulders. He was not afraid, but there were many other tasks he would prefer to undertake with confidence.

Dawn found him waiting at the airport for Nargan's aircraft to arrive. Standing close to the landing area, staring up at the lightening sky above, he waited, wondering what manner of man Nargan would prove to be and how his disguise would suit him. Behind him, on the broad sweep of tarmac in front of the airport buildings, stood the armoured limousine that had been allocated to him.

Bentick straightened up as the plane showed through the clouds and circled the airport gracefully, the rising sun tipping its tapered wings with crimson and silver. As the great plane touched down and ran to a stop, Bentick went on waiting.

Airport officials gathered round the exit hatch in the side of the fuselage. One or two passengers appeared. There were very few on this early plane. Most travellers preferred to make the trip by daylight.

Bentick drifted nearer, moving his hands alternately from his jacket to trouser pockets. He had been told to do this by Cain. Apparently Nargan would recognise him from the signs before he made himself known.

Two men and a woman passed him by without a glance. There was only one other passenger alighting. He was a short, stumpy figure clad in a heavy overcoat and the flat-crowned hat of a scholar. There was white hair showing on either side of his head, and he peered round short-sightedly through pebble-lensed spectacles that magnified his pupils into monstrous orbs. Seeing Bentick, he walked across with a queer kind of shambling gait and halted in front of the agent.

'I want someone to help me find my way round this place,' he announced in a flat, toneless voice. 'You're not doing anything. See to me!'

Bentick took his hands from his pockets. So far so good, he thought. 'Only too glad to oblige,' he said. 'Are your papers in order?'

Nargan, for Nargan it was, gave a brief nod and fumbled in his pocket. He brought out a piece of folded paper and handed it to Bentick, holding it as if he were showing the man an address and asking to be directed there.

Bentick scanned the authority notice narrowly. Yes, he thought, everything was in order. Nargan was wearing the disguise closely described by Cain in his instructions. The authority paper was genuine. Everything was as it should be.

Nargan followed him as he turned and

led the way to the sleek car. The diplomat clutched a briefcase beneath his arm and glanced round before getting inside.

Bentick drove swiftly to the checking office and saw Nargan through the formalities. They were simple enough, for the diplomat was travelling as a business representative from Britain's closest ally in Europe. As a front it was ideal, and Bentick had no misgivings that anything out of the ordinary would arise. Nargan, of course, carried papers that were technically false, but it did not matter under the circumstances.

Once they were clear of the airport, the visitor changed his manner completely. Up till then, Bentick had been thinking that looking after him might not be as bad as he had expected, but Nargan very soon showed himself as he really was.

'Drive faster!' he snapped. 'Do you want some of your revolutionary people to see me and have me assassinated? I'm a very important man at the moment! I shall make my own terms with your country, and in the end we shall bring it to heel as we've always intended!'

Bentick's mouth tightened. Nargan could certainly be unpleasant, he reflected. Oh well, he'd have to put up with that kind of insulting behaviour until the man went home again. It was fortunate that he wouldn't be staying for long. With an effort, Bentick kept his temper under control, smiled, and drove the car faster than before.

'I trust your visit will be satisfactory, Nargan,' he said quietly. 'You'll find our people quite willing to co-operate with you. My country and yours must remain on friendly terms for the sake of international peace.'

Nargan nodded heavily. 'The co-operation will come from you, because you have no choice but to do as I dictate!' he snapped. 'Now stop talking and hurry. I'm tired and filthy from your dirty aircraft! This country appals me!'

Bentick bit back the sharp retort that rose to his lips. No one would thank him for antagonising the man, he thought. This was the very devil!

They continued on the road to Cornwall in silence for a time. Then: 'Where's this hovel to which I am being taken?' demanded the diplomat. 'I was given to understand it's a country house. If it fails to come up to my expectations, I shall return immediately.'

'I think you'll find it suitable,' answered Bentick grimly. 'Everything's been done to make your stay comfortable. Professor Dale won't inconvenience you in any way, and a private suite's been set aside for your own exclusive use while you're there.'

Nargan grunted rudely. Neither man spoke again till Bentick wheeled the car through the rusty gates of Dale's rambling estate on the rugged edge of Cornish moorland. As he drew up in front of the house, Nargan got out and stood for a moment gazing at the building with a sneer on his face. It was an ugly face at the best of times, but now Bentick found it truly repulsive. All the evil of the world might have been there in the brain behind its features.

'A mean place!' said Nargan. He spat on the ground near his feet.

Bentick eyed Dale's home appreciatively. It was a grey stone house nearly five hundred years of age, mellowed by time and weather till the sunlight gleamed silver where it struck and glanced off the sober stone. But Nargan had called it mean. Bentick gave a shrug, turning towards the broad worn steps that led to the massive front door. Nargan followed him with obvious ill grace, glancing from side to side in a short-sighted fashion that, although deceptive, never missed any detail.

Before Bentick could raise a hand to the door, it was opened from inside, swinging back on soundless hinges to reveal a dark-haired woman in a white overall. 'We've been expecting you,' she said quite simply. 'Come in, will you? Professor Dale is busy at the moment, but he asked me to see you comfortably settled.' She broke off, eyeing Bentick gravely.

Bentick smiled and turned to Nargan, but the diplomat was already thrusting past him into the hall. 'I need a bath and a meal at once,' he announced. 'It's a privilege for you to serve me.'

The woman's face altered abruptly at

the words. She glanced at Bentick inquiringly, but he only shook his head slightly in answer to her questioning look. Then she recovered quickly and stepped back to let them through.

As Nargan passed her, he leaned towards her face and showed his teeth in a grin. They were yellow teeth, one of them broken. 'Perhaps my stay in your wretched country won't be as unpleasant as I thought!' he said. His voice was thick and sensuous. Then he patted her on the arm and strode further into the hall.

Bentick, furious at the man's behaviour, was helpless. He saw the anger that flamed on the face of the woman, but to speak to Nargan about his manners would be asking for trouble.

The woman took them up the stairs and threw open the door of a large room, from which a bathroom and smaller bedroom could be reached from inside. 'I hope you'll be comfortable,' she said in a tight voice. 'Everything's ready for you, and I'm given to understand that another visitor's expected at noon tomorrow?'

Nargan gave a nod, stared round the

19

room with a sniff, and slammed the door in Bentick's face. 'Stay within call!' he shouted through the door. 'If I need you, I'll tell you.'

Bentick leant against the wall and rubbed a hand across his forehead. Then his eyes met those of the woman. Quite suddenly they grinned at each other.

'I'm sorry,' whispered Bentick. 'He's in my charge, you know, but I can't very well be responsible for the way he behaves.'

Her face straightened quickly. 'It's not your fault,' she said. She started walking down the corridor, away from Nargan's suite. Bentick hesitated, then followed her.

At the head of the stairs she paused, turning slightly.

'We'd better introduce ourselves,' said Bentick. He told her his name, then waited. This woman impressed him enormously, but he was not quite sure that she was happy. The ghost of a shadow had flitted past her eyes on more than one occasion since he and Nargan had arrived. It was a shadow of fear he had seen, not the distaste that Nargan instilled in her mind. Bentick was curious about her.

'I answer to Carol Collins,' she told him with a smile. 'The professor's my guardian. I work in the laboratory most of the time, and I've got to go back there now. Will you be all right on your own? Just find your way round. I'm afraid there aren't any servants — we can never keep them long.' She grinned cheerily. 'I don't think they like my guardian,' she added. 'He's a strange man. You'll meet him later on.'

Once again Bentick thought he saw the shadow of fear that crossed her face. 'Yes,' he said. 'I'm quite capable of looking after myself. I'll see you again soon, though. Maybe you could show me around when you have the time?'

'I'll be pleased to,' she answered a little stiffly. Then she turned on her heel and walked down the stairs, leaving Bentick at the top with a puzzled frown on his face.

3

The Telecopter

While Bentick was still standing at the head of the stairs wondering about Carol Collins, she had crossed the hall and entered the vast and cavernous kitchen of the house. In the far corner was a closed steel door that looked out of place in a domestic room such as this. She opened it and glanced over her shoulder before going through. Then she was walking along a stone-flagged passage to a flight of steps leading downwards. The passage was lit by naked electric lightbulbs spaced at intervals along its length. It was cold and bare, with a monastic severity that made her shiver slightly, though she had passed this way more times than she could remember.

Beneath the house was a crypt that had been converted by her guardian to a laboratory, in which he spent most of his time. The house stood on the site of an ancient monastery, so the crypt was of even greater age than the building above it. To Carol it was a place of ghosts and the haunting past. Only because loyalty bound her to Dale did she stay there and help him in his work. Sometimes that work frightened her. It did so now, for Dale was a man to whom science was a religion. Nothing was sacred in his eyes but the eternal probing after truth and the hidden things beyond it. Had Bentick realised this, he would have understood the fear that flickered across her eyes as he watched her and talked to her.

The vaulted crypt was a gloomy, mysterious place. Its roof was high and almost lost in the shadows above the glaring lamps that lit it. A gallery ran round its walls on three sides, but this, too, was dark and shrouded in gloom. Masses of complicated apparatus stood on every side, so that almost the entire floor space was occupied by something or other. In the middle of this varied collection was a bent-shouldered figure with snow-white hair and heavy brows.

His features were keen and rugged, but his piercing eyes held a fanatical gleam as he worked.

Carol paused halfway down the steps and watched him for a moment. She reached the point where the steps joined the gallery before continuing down to the floor. Resting one hand on the cold stone balustrade, she hesitated. Professor Dale's latest invention scared her. She was bound to admit that to herself, yet something stronger than her own will kept her there to help him. She was frightened, but had to go on.

Bracing herself, she started down the steps to the floor and walked across to where the professor was working on a machine that might have been some futuristic television set. It stood higher than a person, and had a broad, curving screen that was whitish in colour and opalescent. Below the screen was a complicated switchboard, and rising from above it were massive insulators that capped another maze of electronic equipment.

Dale made an adjustment and straightened up, peering at what he had done.

Only then did he become aware of the woman who was coming towards him. He turned, poking his head out from between his shoulders inquisitively. 'Has our visitor arrived?' he asked in a cracked, high tone of voice. 'I hope he'll be comfortable, my dear!' There was a kind of half-concealed sneer behind the words.

Carol said nothing for a moment. She was fully alive to her guardian's dislike of any outsider who came to the house. What his views on Nargan were she did not know, but had guessed that the diplomat would not be welcome under any circumstances. 'I think they'll be all right,' she answered hesitantly.

'They?' echoed Dale impatiently. 'Am I to understand that there's more than one stranger in my house? I shall get in touch with London at once!'

'There's a second man,' she told him soothingly. 'He's English, and is only here to safeguard the diplomat. They'll both be gone by tomorrow night.' She went to Dale's side, meeting his eyes appealingly. 'Please don't cause a disturbance. The diplomat may be unpleasant, but I understand that so much depends on this meeting that to anger him would be fatal.' Her eyes flamed.

'He's worse than a beast, but I'm ready to be polite for the short time he's here. Don't make it any more difficult than it is already.' He eyed Carol sternly, then shrugged. 'This Nargan is dangerous,' he whispered. 'It's a grave mistake on the part of our government to hand him secrets in exchange for anything. Whatever we give will eventually be used against *us*, not against a common enemy.' As he spoke, his voice rose higher and higher till he was almost shouting.

'Quietly!' said Carol desperately. 'Or he may hear you!'

'I'd like to see him dead!' spat the professor. 'His country is no real friend of ours. They say it'd lead to war if any harm befell him, but I'd sooner see that than the danger ahead if things go on as planned.'

Carol drew away from him, eyes wide with instinctive horror at the thoughts that rose in her mind. She saw madness in the face of Dale, and she knew there was peril in his words. But what could she do? Should she warn Bentick to be on his guard against the very man whose home was the scene of this vital meeting? If she did, it might mean the end of her guardian's scientific research on behalf of Britain. She knew he was a valuable asset, and, although she feared him, she could not quite bring herself to throw any suspicion on him.

She felt helpless and suddenly cowed. All she could do was turn away so as to avoid the gleam in Dale's crazy eyes. To cover her feelings, she changed the subject abruptly. 'Is your invention nearly finished?' she asked in a voice that was none too steady. She gestured with one hand to the apparatus Dale had been working on.

Instantly the scientist was eager. All thoughts of Nargan were swept from his brain, for this machine he was perfecting was the child of his most advanced theories and research. 'It's almost complete!' he told Carol. Turning towards the apparatus lovingly, he laid a hand on its cold steel framework. His fingers touched the dials and switches as if they were made of gold.

'What will you call it?'

'The Telecopter.' He might have been mentioning the name of something sacred. To him, the machine was a deity created by himself.

'Telecopter?' she echoed wonderingly. 'What can a name like that mean? I don't understand.' Although she worked in the laboratory and helped her guardian with most of his experiments, there were many things Professor Dale kept secret. Carol had been watching the growth of his latest invention, but Dale had dropped no hint of its purpose. Now she was genuinely curious, whereas before she had merely been vaguely intrigued as to what it was.

The professor beamed at her shrewdly. His eyes were bright with enthusiasm as he stroked the Telecopter. 'You don't understand? Then perhaps I'll tell you something about it. Quite soon now you'll be able to see some results, but before you do I'll make the idea behind the Telecopter plain to you.'

Carol was conscious of a wave of fear as she listened. There was something uncanny in the professor's voice, as if he were playing with things better left alone. 'Please do,' she said.

Dale stepped away from the machine and stared at it unseeingly for an instant. Then: 'The principle is based on cosmic radiation in the time-space continuum. You must understand that every tiny event that takes place on earth and in the universe sends out emanations in the form of cosmic echoes. These echo waves, as I call them, are circulating through space, and will continue to do so indefinitely. In space, remember, there's nothing to impede their momentum. For as long as the universe continues, those cosmic echoes will be broadcast in perpetual waves that nothing can stop.'

He broke off, his forehead furrowed, deep in thought. Carol licked her lips apprehensively. She said not a word, waiting for Dale to carry on.

'As you know,' he continued, 'I've been experimenting for some time in an attempt to receive these echo waves of past events. The Telecopter is the outcome of my work!'

'But I still don't quite see — '

Dale peered at Carol narrowly. 'You will!' he said in a thin-edged voice. 'You will! With the Telecopter I can show you a clear picture on its screen of anything that happened in this vault since it was dug from the rock.'

Carol nodded dumbly. What Dale spoke of smacked of trickery, yet she knew he was genuine enough in the promises he made, especially where science was concerned. 'Telecopter,' she mused. 'A televising optic that can see back through time. Is that what it means?'

Dale inclined his head gravely. 'You put it as well as I could myself.'

'But I don't see what good it'll be,' protested Carol obstinately. 'How will it benefit people to be able to see into the past? You say it could show what happened in this vault, but what good would that be? I know there was an assassination down here years and years ago, and they say it altered history, but it won't help the world very much even if they could see it happening exactly as it did.'

Dale smiled pityingly. 'My child, there's much you don't understand. At the moment I admit that the Telecopter can only show events as they happened in the exact spot on which it stands, but in time I shall perfect it so that not only will it produce an image of some happening in any part of the world, but I hope to advance my work to such an extent that the *future* will also be visible before it occurs. You must realise, of course, that even events that have not yet happened are already foreshadowed in the fabric of space. If I can gather them in and translate them onto the screen, then nothing will be hidden from me.' He paused, watching her closely. Then: 'I have every hope that the Telecopter in its present form will see beyond the moment in which we're living. It should be able to receive near-future events, at any rate, and by tonight I'll know if my work has been successful!'

Carol stared at the machine in awe. Somehow the notion of being able to see future events was horrible. To see the past re-enacted would be bad enough, besides being a waste of time; but to see the future before it happened — ! Her mind boggled at the very idea of it.

Professor Dale went on watching her. 'You don't believe me, do you, my child? Well, I'll prove it to you shortly. When such an incredible advance as this is made by science, it's something that no man can keep to himself! Others must share the triumph!'

Carol found she could say nothing. She wanted to be alone, to have time to think. She wished there were someone to whom she could talk in a sane manner. She thought of Bentick somewhere upstairs. He looked like a straight-thinking man, and an honest one, but she had no right to trouble him with this kind of worry. Besides, she still felt a certain loyalty towards Dale in spite of the dread and fear he put in her mind.

She managed to smile a little, but could not bring herself to look the professor full in the eyes when she did it. 'It sounds . . . exciting,' she said. 'I — I hope it works as well as you expect.' She broke off, searching for an excuse to escape. 'I must go upstairs again now. Our visitors will want a meal.' She turned and hurried from the crypt without another word.

4

Confidences

Professor Dale stood against the Telecopter, one hand on its smooth steel case, fingers drumming as his eyes followed Carol's figure across the floor of the vault and up the steps to the gallery before she disappeared. Then he shrugged and turned back to his work, poring over detailed plans that lay on a littered bench.

Carol reached the big kitchen at the end of the stone passage and halted abruptly. Grinning at her cheerfully from the other side of the room was Bentick, a frying pan in one hand and a plate of bacon in the other.

'Hello,' he said before she could find her voice. 'I hope you won't mind, but you did say I should find my own way round.' He broke off and jerked his head towards the door. 'My charge is getting hungry,' he added. 'I've discovered that when that happens he becomes difficult to handle.'

Carol relaxed. This man was refreshing, she thought. There was something very solid and reliable about him. She liked him instinctively. 'So you started cooking,' she laughed. 'I'm terribly sorry, but I've just left the laboratory to come and look after you. You'll have to forgive us, Mr. Bentick, but we aren't an awfully hospitable household I'm afraid. At least, my guardian isn't, which makes it rather difficult for me.'

He looked at her sharply for a second, as her unhappiness was apparent in her words. He would have liked to do something to help her, but thrusting himself into her life was something he could not do. If she needed help, the seeking must come from her. Aloud he said: 'For heaven's sake, don't worry about it. I'm perfectly capable of fending for myself if you're busy. This job isn't a pleasant one, but it's got to be done, so I'm ready to make the best of it.' He gave her a rueful smile and set down the frying pan as she came across.

'This man, Nargan,' she began; 'the

professor told me something about him. He's important, isn't he? I don't envy you your work. He's so unpleasant.'

Bentick eyed her shrewdly. 'I'll be frank: I hate the man. He was insufferable to you, but I couldn't do anything about it at the time. If I ever have the chance, I'll pay him back in kind; but until this business is over, I'm afraid I've just got to toe the line and watch his disgusting behaviour.' He smiled. 'For the good of the country, you understand. For continued peace on earth.'

She looked away quickly. 'I know that.' After a pause, she said: 'Here, let me do the cooking!' She was suddenly bright with a forced cheerfulness that was almost painful to watch.

Bentick stood aside. 'Professor Dale is a busy man?' he queried presently. 'What's he doing at the moment? Something fantastic as usual?' His words were light and easy.

Carol turned and met his gaze. There was the same shadow of fear behind her eyes that he'd seen before. It troubled him.

'I'm scared,' she confessed. 'I don't quite know why, but I am. It — it's like witchcraft or something. Seeing into the past and the future. Oh, it's horrible!'

'Maybe it'd help to tell me about it. I don't want to hurt your feelings, but I've heard that Dale's a little eccentric at times.'

'Yes, he is. This latest invention of his, the Telecopter he calls it, can make an image of past events as well as seeing into the future. Can you imagine looking at a picture of what hasn't happened yet? That's what scares me so! And he's dangerous as well. Things he's said about the man you're with — things that frightened me.' She stared at Bentick with widened eyes, afraid now that she'd said too much.

Bentick looked at her thoughtfully. 'You'd better be perfectly honest with me,' he told her. 'If there's anything going on, or likely to happen, that in any way endangers this man I'm guarding, it's up to you to tell me about it.'

'Professor Dale is fanatical about him,' she whispered. 'He told me he wishes

Nargan were dead, and when he said it there was something in his eyes that disturbed me. It can't be connected with the Telecopter, of course, but it's all very worrying.' She shivered suddenly, then tilted her head to one side, listening. From somewhere far below their feet came the muted hum of machinery starting up. It rose to an eerie whine and steadied on a high-pitched note that was faint but insistent. Bentick raised an eyebrow inquiringly.

'The generators,' Carol whispered. 'That means he's using power now. He'll want it to test the Telecopter, so it looks as if he's completed it. He's probably seeing things on the screen even now — things that have happened in that vault. Perhaps even things that *will* happen down there!'

Bentick decided that the time had come to take some definite action. His feelings were torn between loyalty and the need to help Carol. And always there was Nargan in the background, an evil shadow if ever there was one. 'You and I might be able to assist each other,' he said. 'I don't want to pry into your affairs or those of Professor Dale, but we must co-operate.'

She looked at him curiously. 'What do you mean? I can't show you secret things, if that's what you want. They're not mine to show.'

'I don't want you to. But keep me informed of any developments that might affect my own particular job; that's all I ask. It's important that personal loyalties are put aside in a matter like this. You can, of course, have complete confidence in my discretion.'

'All right,' she breathed. 'I'll do that. It isn't nice to spy on people you know so well, but I'll keep an eye on my guardian just in case he shows signs of becoming dangerous towards Nargan. In return, I know I can rely on you if I need any help myself.'

Bentick would have said a lot more had there not been an interruption. The door of the kitchen burst open and Nargan appeared, his sallow face creased in a frown that made Bentick remember his duty with a guilty start.

'Where's my food?' demanded the diplomat angrily. 'Am I to be starved as well as insulted in your cursed country? I've been here but a short time, yet already I hate the place and find it humiliating to a man of my position and importance. And what about acting as my bodyguard? You're worthless! I've been left to myself. My calls have gone unanswered, although I told you to stay within hearing!' He broke off and shook his fist at Bentick. 'I shall have you broken for this!' he shouted. 'The miserable men who employ you will hear about your complete disregard for my safety! You're negligent!'

Bentick contained his anger as best he could. 'I only left you to get your food,' he said.

Nargan snorted. 'What's the woman for? To be an amusing ornament?'

'She was busy with other things,' said Bentick through clenched teeth. 'Everything's ready now. If you'll go to the dining room, you can satisfy your hunger.'

Carol, too furious and injured to trust her voice, kept quiet. Bentick was glad, for he felt she would only have made matters worse by speaking. Taking advantage of the lull, he urged Nargan from the kitchen and took him along to the front of the house, where a table was laid in a sunny room.

Carol followed them, a tray in her hands. She said not a word as she served them, but when Bentick caught her eye she was looking far from pleased. Nargan, brightening up considerably since the scene he had caused in the kitchen, made several remarks that made her flush before she could escape, and Bentick cursed the circumstances that prevented him from giving the man the hiding he deserved.

Their meal over, Nargan pushed back his chair and rose from the table. 'I shall return to my room now,' he announced.

Bentick nodded gratefully. 'I'll be around,' he said. 'You need have no fear of danger in this house. These people are as loyal as anyone could wish. I'll call you at lunchtime if that's convenient. In the meantime, I won't be far away.'

'Don't leave the house!' snapped Nargan.

'There's no one I can trust in this country. Too many people hate me for what I do — but soon I shall bring you all to heel, as is fitting for a lesser nation!'

Bentick watched venomously as the diplomat strutted from the room and thumped his way up the stairs with ponderous steps. Then he shrugged and wandered thoughtfully towards the kitchen, hoping that Carol might be there. When he reached it, however, there was no sign of her. He halted, staring curiously at the steel door that opened the way to the vault and laboratory. He knew that was where it led because Carol had come through it when she found him in the kitchen earlier on. There was something very intriguing about that door. Almost against his better judgment he moved towards it, drawn by curiosity and a desire to know what lay beyond. The high-pitched note of the hidden generator was still singing in his ears. He wondered if Nargan had noticed it.

Before he could bring himself to open the door, however, someone did it for him from the other side. Bentick found himself staring into the pale face of Carol as she stood in the opening, watching him with slightly parted lips.

'Hello,' he said. 'I was hoping I'd see you; that's why I came here.'

She recovered her composure quickly. 'The professor sent me up for something,' she explained. 'He's already had results from the Telecopter. I haven't seen them myself because he switched it off as soon as I went down, but I can tell something's happened. There's a kind of excitement in the way he speaks and looks at me with his eyes. It makes me frightened!'

'Anything I can do to help?'

She shook her head slowly. 'I don't think so. I'm all right. Is Nargan happy now?'

Bentick grinned. 'He's probably sleeping off his breakfast by now! He's the biggest swine I've met in years, but it can't be helped. Frankly I'll be very glad when tomorrow's over and done, except that I may not see you again.'

Carol dropped her gaze at his words. They were standing close together on the stone-flagged floor of the kitchen. They were still like that when a figure appeared in the open steel door and halted, peering at them narrowly with an impish expression on his face. It was Dale, head poked forward and white overall coat crumpled and stained. Bentick jerked his head up and met the professor's gaze. It was the first time he had seen the man, and now he realised something of the fanaticism that drove him through life.

'Good morning,' said Dale in a voice that was little more than a croak. 'I don't like visitors in my house, as Carol has probably told you, and I like this Nargan less than most; but I understand that his presence here is not your doing, young man. You're as welcome as anyone would be under the circumstances . . . which is not a great deal.' He paused, going on before Bentick could speak: 'But I forget myself! I came to find Carol, as the time has come when I can't keep my secrets hidden any longer.'

Carol stared at him wordlessly for an instant. She had instinctively moved a little further away from Bentick, but now she edged closer to his side again.

Bentick said: 'I hope your experiments

44

are going successfully, Professor. You've been a greater benefactor to scientific advancement than any other living man. Is it too much to ask what your latest developments will mean to humanity?' He made a gesture. 'Please don't think me inquisitive.'

Dale grinned in a peculiarly wolfish fashion. 'Of course you're inquisitive,' he said. 'It's a human trait. If I weren't inquisitive, I wouldn't do the things I do. No man would!'

Bentick did not quite know what to say to that, so kept quiet. Dale went on: 'You're inquisitive! Of course you are. And I'm sufficiently human myself to want to boast about what I've achieved. You and Carol shall see the results of my work!'

Carol gave a little gasp. Bentick frowned, puzzled.

'Come along down to the laboratory, both of you,' said Dale. It was more of a command than an invitation. 'You'll see things there that no one other than myself has had the privilege to see. I'll show you the past — but not the dead past, my friends! I've brought the past to life in an image! And I shall bring the future into being in the same fashion. Follow me!'

Carol looked at Bentick as the professor turned and started through the steel door again. Bentick gave her a smile of encouragement, but he was conscious of a quickening of his pulses as he realised that Dale meant to demonstrate the Telecopter to them. He should have felt proud to be included in the invitation, but instead he wondered whether the things that this man was doing were wise.

Following the professor closely, the two of them entered the passage beyond the door and walked in Dale's wake as the scientist led them along. Not once did the man glance back to see if they were coming; he took it for granted that they would. At the head of the gallery steps overlooking the vault, however, he halted, turning to Carol.

'Prepare yourself,' he said tensely. 'You're about see the shadows of events that in their time have altered the history of this country!'

As they descended the steps to the floor

of the laboratory, Bentick stared round, fascinated. Dale's eyes were fixed on the Telecopter as he went towards it. There was a loving care in the way he fingered the switches as the other two watched him.

5

Past and Future

'Switch the lights off, my dear,' said Dale to Carol.

Bentick noticed then that there were electric light switches on the wall behind her. She turned and operated them so that the laboratory was in almost total darkness. Only a pilot light on the Telecopter machine glowed ruddily, eerily illuminating Professor Dale's features. Carol, having turned the lights off as she was bidden, shrank against Bentick in the gloom. He caught a glimpse of her face, a small white blur at his shoulder. Her whole attention was riveted on the Telecopter.

'Now!' breathed Dale. 'Now you'll see!'

The large opalescent screen of the machine glowed with a bluish flicker, then steadied to a more even light between blue and green. Flashes crossed it at intervals. As they did so, the professor was mumbling to himself, the presence of his audience completely forgotten.

Suddenly the screen changed. Dale bent closer to the front, his fingers working fast on the controls as he sought for what he wanted. Bentick, fascinated by the whole business, stared till his eyes ached with the strain. There was darkness on the screen for an instant. When it cleared, he saw what appeared to be figures moving here and there as if seen through a mist. Carol, at his side, caught her breath in a whisper of something close to fear.

Dale made further adjustments to the machine. He was lost to all other considerations beyond his own achievements. The figures on the screen became clear, turning from shadows to people. It might have been a film of some scene in history. Bentick was not very sure of his facts, but he thought the clothes they wore belonged to the Tudor period. And then he noticed another curious thing: the setting of the image was none other than the vault in which they all stood so tensely. Everything was there: the stone floor, the steps to the gallery with its heavy balustrade, the vaulted roof partially lost in gloom. All that was missing was the jumble of modern apparatus that filled the place now.

Dale broke in on his thoughts. Still gazing at the image on the Telecopter screen, he said: 'A scene from history! A scene enacted here in this very place hundreds of years ago, and brought to life by the eyes of the Telecopter! Eyes that can see through the past and into the future! Is it not incredible? And *I* have created this wonder!'

'It's certainly amazing, Professor,' murmured Bentick cautiously. 'What is that picture? Do you know?' As he spoke, he was watching the moving figures on the screen. There were seven of them, all men. They moved stealthily, gathering together in a group in the centre of the big crypt floor. There they stood, heads together, sometimes glancing across their shoulders as if fearing an interruption.

Dale said: 'You may know from history that the assassination of a famous man was planned within these very walls. What you see now at this moment is the cosmic reflection of the actual meeting. Had it not been for that meeting, and the plans that were laid by the men you can see before you, this nation would never have been as great as it is. History would've taken a different course, and England might well have fallen.'

Bentick could not help but feel a sense of awe as he watched and listened. It was true that he had heard of the grim events that Dale had spoken of. But to see them taking place — ! It was almost beyond comprehension. Aloud he said: 'Where did the actual murder occur?'

'Down here, where you stand,' answered the professor calmly. 'I'll show you presently. I've not yet completely mastered the technique of searching time for the events I wish to see. But later I shall be adept at the game!'

Bentick tried to tear his eyes from the screen of the Telecopter but found it almost impossible. His mind was being instilled with the sensation of conspiracy that obviously enthralled the men whose images he saw. It was as if the very fact of seeing that picture was drawing his soul into it; drawing him back through time till he felt he was a part of that scene. It was uncanny, yet he could not fight against it.

Only a sudden whisper from Carol succeeded in shaking him out of the past. 'He must die!' she breathed. 'It will be for England that he dies!'

Bentick shivered at the sound of her words. He made a superhuman effort and turned to look at her. In the dim light her face was expressionless, her eyes fixed on the screen as his own had been. Her lips were moving, but she seemed to be in a kind of trance, as if her mind were no longer her own.

'Turn that thing off, Professor!' said Bentick sharply. 'Miss Collins isn't well. There's something queer about your Telecopter. Turn it off!'

Dale seemed to stiffen at the words. He turned reluctantly as Bentick finished speaking, and his hand reached out and cut the master switches. The screen went dead and blank. At the same time, Bentick flicked the electric light switches, and the laboratory was flooded with brilliance. He felt strangely thankful that everything was the same as it had been. He was almost afraid of the effect that shimmering screen had had on his mind. There was something evil about it; and Dale, too, now became a figure of indefinable menace.

'What did you say?' demanded Dale. 'Carol not well? I don't understand! She looks all right to me!'

Bentick glanced sideways at her. She was looking round dazedly. Then she shook herself violently and smiled at the professor. 'Of course I'm all right!' she said brightly. 'Just a slight touch of dizziness, that's all.'

Dale grunted, but Bentick eyed her curiously. There was something queer about the Telecopter, he thought. He'd have to keep an eye on things or there'd be trouble of some kind before long. Dale, he decided, was very close to insanity. Maybe a tactful word to Cain when he got back to London might come in useful. Carol should not be left with Dale, in any event.

But before he could say a word, and before Dale could open his mouth to speak again, there was a shout from the top of the gallery steps. It was Nargan, demanding to know what on earth Bentick thought he was doing by deserting his post when at any moment there might be danger from some hidden quarter. The agent hesitated. He was on the point of making a furious retort, but saw the futility of it before it was too late.

Professor Dale smiled vindictively. 'Your friend appears to be a man of short temper and bad manners,' he said smoothly. 'I think perhaps you'd better look after him.' In an undertone he added: 'Get him out of here at all costs!' There was a threat in his tone that Bentick was quick to heed. In a moment he had hurried to the steps and was running up them to the gallery where Nargan waited, too angry to take much notice of his surroundings.

Bentick had all his work cut out to soothe the diplomat sufficiently to lead him quietly back to his own part of the house; and when eventually he did so, he realised he ought not to leave him again, at least until he was asleep that night. But thoughts of Carol alone with Professor Dale and the Telecopter troubled the agent. He was determined to see her again as soon as he could.

Meanwhile, Carol was still in the laboratory with the professor. She was shaken by her experience of watching the Telecopter screen, but gave no sign of it to her guardian. Dale, on the other hand, was curious about her in a strangely analytical fashion. Although he had said there was nothing wrong with her, he had sensed something of the things she had experienced. He began to feel that his latest invention might have even greater possibilities than he had hitherto visualised. Carol was his guinea pig, and he did not mean to lose her.

While he busied himself at his bench, studying plans and occasionally making a minor adjustment to the Telecopter, his mind was working along hidden paths. When he finally spoke to Carol, his voice was mild to the point of being gentle. 'You like the young man upstairs, don't you, my dear? He's certainly good-looking. I think perhaps you're a little in love with him already.'

Carol tossed her head. 'Don't be absurd!' she snapped. 'I hardly know him! He hasn't been in the house more than a few hours.'

Dale smiled knowingly. 'Perhaps not,' he mused. 'Perhaps not, child, but I wonder what the future could tell us. I really do wonder sometimes, you know.'

Carol caught her breath and bit her lower lip. She was afraid of Dale and his Telecopter. But she kept silent, watching the professor doubtfully. He moved across to the machine again, smiling to himself in a sinister manner that filled her with fear.

'Yes,' he murmured softly. 'Yes, I really do wonder what the future could hold. Shall we try to find out?'

'No!' The single word was wrung from Carol's lips as if to ward off some nameless peril.

Dale turned and eyed her steadily. 'You're a little fool. When a man gives his soul to science, nothing must stand in his way! Do you understand? Nothing!'

Carol swallowed painfully. 'I must go

upstairs,' she said shakily. 'I — I don't feel very well just now. Please let me go!'

Dale rounded on her sharply. 'You shall go when I'm ready to do without an assistant! Until then, you'll stay here and watch the screen.'

Fighting a desire to turn and run, Carol stayed where she was.

'Turn the lights out!' Dale ordered curtly.

Carol did as she was told without protest. Dale's will was too strong to resist, but she would have been far happier in her own mind had Bentick been there to give her courage. But he was somewhere upstairs with his noxious charge, probably being told off in an ill-mannered fashion for neglecting his duty as a guard. Despite her own troubles, Carol felt sorry for him.

In the darkness of the laboratory, the Telecopter screen suddenly glowed with its bluish light. Dale worked the switches and controls, and the screen was obscured by a series of flickering lines and circles. Then they, too, were wiped aside and a recognisable image appeared in their place.

Carol gasped as she realised that what she was seeing on the screen was the present moment. The illumination was so dim as to be almost nonexistent, but she saw herself standing there, just as she was, staring into the screen. She could also see the professor as he bent towards the Telecopter, partially obscuring her view. Compelled by something stronger than her own will to see all she could, she moved in closer. Her image on the screen did likewise.

Dale said: 'The present, you see, child! There's nothing frightening in that, now, is there?'

'No,' she said, still uncertain of her feelings.

'Shall we go further, then?' Dale did not wait for an answer, but flicked his fingers over the dials and stared at the screen. From a white shimmering blankness, it changed by slow degrees till once again a figure was revealed.

'This is the future!' whispered Dale in excited tones. 'Do you hear that, Carol? You're looking at the future!'

Carol was looking at an image of herself. She appeared to be alone. There was a faint light in the vault, and every detail was recognisable.

'This is happening not very far ahead of us,' said Dale. 'See, you're wearing the same clothes as you are at this moment!' The excitement rose in his voice as Carol on the screen started moving and turning her head. On the pictured face there was fear and doubt. Then suddenly she was screaming, hiding her face with her hands.

The Carol of the present gave a gasp of dismay as she saw what would happen in the future. Fear rose within her, for the terror on that imaged face of hers filled her heart with dread. 'Stop it!' she cried. 'Stop it, I tell you!'

But Dale kept the picture in focus with relentless determination, dividing his attention between the screen and the woman, watching for signs and reactions. He felt the fear that was in the air; it seemed to emanate from the Telecopter and reach out towards him. Only with difficulty did he fight it down.

But Carol was breaking. She felt the fullness of terror that sprang from her own image. The scream that would one day be coming from her own lips was there now for her eyes to see. She sobbed and tried to bury her face, but the power of the Telecopter to hold its audience was far too strong.

The Carol on the screen was staring fixedly at something just beyond the range of vision of the machine. She would have given anything to know what that something was. Then another figure obscured the picture, crossing it with its back in view. It was a dark figure, stealthy-looking and quite unrecognisable. It went towards Carol's image, but before it reached her Dale cut the switches suddenly.

'Turn on the lights!' he snapped. 'I don't want to drive you mad, my child.'

Shuddering violently, Carol obeyed. She had no strength of her own, or so it seemed.

'You've seen into the future,' Dale repeated. 'What's written in the cosmos must come to pass. A moment will come when terror will visit you here in this spot!'

6

Nargan is Curious

Carol was filled with panic as she listened to Dale's words. Silently she turned on her heel and fled from the vault, running up the steps as if a fiend were close on her tail. It was not the professor himself she was so terrified of, but the things he had shown her; the things that were there in her destiny and would inevitably happen.

Dale watched her go but made no attempt to stop her. His face was alive with the success of the Telecopter. He had achieved the seemingly impossible, and could now foretell the future. Later on, he thought, the range of his latest invention would be increased so that events outside its immediate vicinity would be readily visible. His brain reeled at the vast possibilities thus opened up. In a short while he could make himself master of the world by taking advantage of his own foreknowledge, turning the future to his own ends and those of his country; for he had not yet forsaken the interests of his native land.

Meanwhile, Carol, reaching the kitchen and finding it empty, ran straight on and up the stairs to the privacy of her own room. She dare not face anything or anybody in her present state of mind, and was glad that Bentick was not around to see her. As if bolts and bars could keep out terror, she locked herself in and flung herself on the bed, hiding from the things that haunted her, yet never losing them completely. Nothing, she felt, could wipe out the fear that sat in her heart when she remembered those relentlessly vivid pictures that Dale had shown her.

And while Carol lay stiff and rigidly afraid in her room, Bentick and Nargan were close at hand in the diplomat's suite; while below in the gloomy laboratory, Professor Dale was probing the future with the eyes of the Telecopter. The things he saw there put fresh thoughts into his fevered mind and set him working eagerly to establish further facts.

Upstairs, Nargan was in an odd frame of mind. He gave Bentick a trying time for quite a while after fetching him up from the vault, but as soon as his temper was spent his manner changed abruptly. He was curious.

Bentick sensed the change and distrusted it. He even had an inkling of what would be the outcome of any investigation by the diplomat into the professor's doings, and was determined at all costs to prevent it.

Nargan opened by remarking on the well-kept secrets of Dale's laboratory. 'Behind a steel door and secret passages!' He chuckled. 'The steel door was left open when I came to find you. That's no way to guard a secret, my friend!'

Bentick eyed him suspiciously, guessing that this was the start of a probe into Dale's activities. 'It's none of my business how Dale guards his secrets,' he said. 'I was only in the lab by chance. Carol took me down.'

Nargan's eyes were steely. 'So you're not aware of what the professor is working on? I can hardly believe that! It seems strange for a brilliant scientist to let outsiders watch him at work — unless, of course, he's demonstrating something new and original especially for their benefit.' He watched Bentick closely as he spoke, seeking for some reaction that would give him a clue to what he wanted to know.

But Bentick was cagey. 'Professor Dale wasn't demonstrating anything,' he answered briefly. 'I know nothing of his affairs beyond the fact that in the past he's produced a great deal of valuable work on behalf of my country. He'll no doubt continue to do so, but I assume that he keeps his secrets intact from popular curiosity. He's reticent even with Carol, who acts as his assistant, so it's highly unlikely that he'd divulge anything important to a stranger, don't you think?'

Nargan nodded wisely. 'Perhaps we shall see later on,' he murmured. 'I'm a man who's willing to drive a bargain to a point where refusal would be fatal. If Dale is concerned about the well-being of his country, I shall bring him to heel as I've done to others in the past.'

Bentick did not deign to answer. He realised, however, that Nargan's curiosity would be a dangerous factor with which to contend. He did not feel inclined to approach the professor on the subject, yet he felt that something should be done to put him on his guard. If he could have a word with Carol, she might be able to help.

But Nargan was not co-operative in letting him go for a long while. He questioned Bentick closely about all manner of different things. Only by using all his wits did the agent avoid falling into traps skilfully laid by the diplomat. By the end of an hour, Bentick was hating Nargan more intensely than he had ever hated a man in his life before. Under the cloak of apparent friendship, the diplomat was trying as hard as he could to milk Bentick's brain for information. But Bentick came through the ordeal with a feeling that he had given nothing of importance away during their trying conversation. All the same, he knew he would be very glad when his task was completed and Nargan gone from England's shores.

Midday had come and gone before Bentick finally broke away, with the excuse of finding out what arrangements had been made for lunch. It struck him that this was the queerest visit he had ever paid to a country home. He and Nargan might have been alone in the house for all the interest shown by Professor Dale; and Carol was fully occupied with other matters.

While Bentick was nosing round the house in search of her, Nargan was doing some furious thinking. It seemed to him that unless he took a few risks, he might well miss something that would prove to be vital. Although at the time of his hasty visit to the laboratory he had not taken in any details of the various apparatus, he now remembered that the three people down there had been gathered round one particular piece in attitudes of intense interest and concentration.

Nargan was determined to find out what that apparatus was. Nothing, he decided, would prevent him from doing so. For all he knew, it might be some new weapon invented by Dale for use by

Britain against his own country in the event of war. To gain foreknowledge of its potential would be the greatest stroke in his career, and a stroke which might one day prove invaluable in bringing this country down, as he had every intention of doing.

Bentick, finding no trace of Carol in the kitchen or other open rooms of the house, assumed she must be in the laboratory. To save trouble for everyone concerned, he rustled up some food and took it to the dining room, then went to Nargan and told him that everything was ready.

The diplomat, from behind a locked door, shouted out to say that he was having a bath and would be down in about an hour's time. The food, he added, could not be made worse by waiting till he was ready.

Bentick sighed and gave a rueful grin. Nargan was certainly not the kind to make friends among the people he met. He wandered down the stairs and found his way to the library. There was no one there, so he sat and read a paper, trying to still the doubts in his mind and forget Nargan for a time.

But the diplomat was not having a bath. That had been nothing but a blind, as were most of the things he did. The moment Bentick had walked away down the corridor, Nargan had crept to his door and listened carefully. Then he, too, was moving towards the stairs and making his way down to the ground floor.

Bentick, after reading for a few minutes and finding he could not concentrate, sat staring through the window at the rolling waste of moors outside. He was still sitting there when Professor Dale came in, his white coat stained and crumpled, and hair awry. Without a word to Bentick he crossed to the sideboard and poured himself a stiff drink, which he downed at a gulp. Only then did he turn and acknowledge the young man who had risen from his chair and stood watching him a trifle guiltily.

'So you've made yourself comfortable, I see!' grunted the scientist. 'I wish people wouldn't make so free of my house. If I'd known what that Nargan fellow was going to be like, I should never have agreed to his coming here for any meeting — even an important one!'

'I'm sorry about it, sir,' said Bentick. 'I know it must be unpleasant for you, but it's for the good of our country.'

'I wonder if it is,' mused Dale. His eyes were glinting brightly as he spoke. 'It might be, of course. I might be able to turn the bad into good. We shall see!'

Bentick was on the point of saying something else when Dale swung on his heel and left the room again. He started to follow the professor, intending to ask where Carol was, but in the end decided not to and sat down in the chair again, frowning in a puzzled fashion.

Professor Dale hurried back through the kitchen. At the steel door to the laboratory, however, he halted abruptly, his face suddenly pale with tension. The door stood ajar. Dale knew he had closed it behind him when he came up for a drink. Then his eyes narrowed as he remembered Nargan. Sucking in his breath between his teeth with a venomous hiss, he slipped quietly through the door and made his way along the passage to the head of the broad gallery steps. There he stopped again, looking down at the laboratory and smiling gently to himself.

What he saw was Nargan down there. And Nargan was bending forward, staring at the Telecopter with an intensity of purpose that quickly told Dale the man was out to probe its secrets.

Very quietly, the scientist advanced down the steps from the gallery till he stood at their foot and watched Nargan. The diplomat had not yet realised he was no longer alone. His hand reached out to the switches of the Telecopter in an effort to bring something to life on the mysterious screen before him, but before he could succeed in doing anything Professor Dale gave a cough and started walking towards him. Instantly Nargan whirled, his hand flashing down to one of his pockets where he kept his gun.

Professor Dale ignored the threat of the gun as he faced the diplomat. 'So I have another visitor!' he said with a gently disarming smile. 'I'm always pleased to entertain guests, my friend. Was there anything in particular you wished to see?'

Nargan was somewhat taken aback by this reception. He had expected furious anger on the part of the professor at his intrusion where he was not wanted, but this was something entirely different. At first he did not know quite how to handle the situation, but his quick-acting brain soon grasped the position and gave his tongue the glibness it was used to.

'Ah, my dear professor!' He beamed. 'Please do forgive me for coming down here uninvited, but I wished to locate that excellent young man who's acting as my bodyguard. He mentioned having been here, and I thought to find him again. An interesting place you have, yes? There are many wonderful things to delight the eyes of a scientist. I wish I had your knowledge and ability with this apparatus.'

Dale gave a thin-lipped smile. He was in no way deceived by Nargan's silky tones, and was already forming a plan to discomfit the man. If Nargan wished to probe, he should have his money's worth, he thought. Aloud he said: 'I'm only too delighted to oblige you by revealing a few of my secrets. They are, of course, something I must trust you never to pass on to anyone else, but I know you won't fail me. While I understand that you have the interests of your own country at heart, I'm also aware that you're a friend of England, and as such would never betray a trust.'

Nargan bowed his head, concealing the flush of satisfaction that rose to his cheeks at Dale's simple words. The man might be clever, but he was certainly a fool to trust anyone, let alone himself, the most cunning of men! 'You're too kind, Professor,' he murmured. 'I'm a man of faith myself, as you must've heard. Whatever you show me will remain locked in my mind, safe from danger.'

Dale gave a matter-of-fact nod. 'I understand,' he said more briskly. He indicated the Telecopter. 'Now this piece of apparatus is my latest development. I haven't yet perfected it, or probed its full potential, but you shall see me demonstrate it in spite of that.'

As he talked, he was operating the controls of the Telecopter. He then gave

Nargan a brief and lucid description of the principles on which the machine worked and described the results it gave. When he mentioned its ability to see into the future, Nargan realised he was on to something of the utmost value.

Dale turned the lights out and started the Telecopter, showing Nargan pictures from the past as they had happened in the vault years before. Nargan saw the same group of conspirators as Bentick had seen. He was convinced of Dale's genuineness by this brief demonstration, for there was no denying the proof the scientist gave him of the efficacy of the machine.

Dale paused, leaving the screen blank for a moment. 'Not only can the Telecopter reveal the past,' he said, 'but the future is also available at will. Watch!'

Nargan, in a fever of excitement, kept his eyes on the screen as Dale brought light to its shimmering surface again. The next moment the professor was showing him an image of Carol screaming in terror. Now Nargan himself became aware of fear for the first time. His bulky frame went rigid.

Dale, fighting for control over his own emotions and keeping his eyes from the screen, changed abruptly in manner. 'That's written in the future!' he whispered with a remorseless hate in his words. 'That woman you see will scream in terror, and do you know why? Because she'll see *you* die! That's your own doom foreshadowed, Nargan! Nothing can prevent it; nothing can alter the destiny that rules our lives. The terror of death is in her and in you!'

7

Spy by Night

With a supreme effort, Nargan gained some control of his fear. His sallow face was patchy and grey, and his lips quivered, but now he was angry as well as frightened. 'You shall pay for this trickery, Dale!' he whispered in a barely audible voice. 'There's nothing but trickery in your brain. Tricks that can frighten for a moment or two, but have no real power over life!'

Dale gave a shrug, but his face was crinkled in a thin smile that was like a mask of venom. The madness in his eyes gleamed fiercely, yet he appeared perfectly calm. When he spoke again, his words were cool and level. 'I don't indulge in cheap trickery, Nargan,' he said. 'What you've seen is the shadow of destiny. Nothing you or I can do will alter it. I think perhaps you'd better leave me now. I have work to do.'

Nargan, still frightened and angry, turned on his heel and hastened from the laboratory without a backward glance. He knew in his heart that Dale had been speaking the truth. And the truth was a terrifying thing. Had he thought otherwise, he would willingly have killed Dale where he stood, but he knew it would not save his own skin if the things the scientist had said were true. And Nargan knew they were.

He arrived back in the kitchen with a troubled frown on his face and shaky nerves, a very unusual thing for such a hardened man. There he came across Bentick, who was roaming about in search of something. The two men stared at each other for an instant before either spoke. Then Nargan began by chastising Bentick as severely as he could.

'I've had to wander about this cursed house to find you!' he shouted furiously. 'Why are you never on hand when I want you? This matter will be reported to your superiors, just as others will be. I'm going to break you, and watch it happen!'

Bentick kept his temper with difficulty. It took all his reserves of tact to handle Nargan, and even then he was never sure that the man was mollified. He was like an ever-hungry devil. And Bentick could sense that he was frightened of something as well, though it was concealed behind a facade of anger.

'You've been in the laboratory?' he said. 'I hope it proved interesting, but I hardly expected the professor to show you around *there*!'

Nargan drew himself up. His bulky figure seemed to tower suddenly. 'Dale will do exactly as I wish!' he snapped. 'I've nothing more to say on the matter. And if I can't find you when I need you again, there will be further trouble. From now until your country's representative arrives here tomorrow, I'll be in my room, and shall not leave it. You or the woman will bring my meals to me there.'

Bentick nodded slowly. To be honest, he felt quite relieved at the news. He could not guess what Dale had shown Nargan to frighten him so much. It might be the Telecopter, he thought, yet it seemed unlikely that the professor would do such a thing under the circumstances — unless, of course, he had some ulterior motive behind the action. Bentick was worried as he watched Nargan strut from the kitchen and disappear.

Soon he decided to continue his search for Carol. He felt he had a sufficient excuse for finding her, as he could pass on the latest news about Nargan. There was still no sign of her in the lower part of the house, so he took his courage in both hands and tried some of the bedroom doors on the upper floor. One he found to be locked, and he gave the panel a tap.

Carol came to the door and opened it quietly and a little fearfully, but when she saw Bentick her face cleared at once. He noted the dark shadows under her eyes and realised she was worried out of her wits about something.

'Hello!' he said lightly. 'What's the trouble? I've been looking for you.'

'Have you? I've been meaning to come and talk to you, but I didn't have the courage.' Her eyes were appealing as she met his steady gaze.

'Come downstairs for a minute. We can talk in peace there.'

She shook her head. 'Nargan might be listening,' she whispered. 'Come in here. There are things I feel I have to tell you, but I'm frightened.'

Bentick did not speak, but followed her in through the open door of her room. He glanced round automatically, noting its tidiness and the charm of the furnishings. He could also tell from the rumpled condition of the bed that Carol must have flung herself full-length on the cover and stayed there for quite a long time.

She turned and faced him near the open window. 'That awful machine the professor calls the Telecopter,' she said. 'There's something evil about it.'

Bentick nodded thoughtfully. 'Yes, I know. I felt it myself. Have you had another chance to see what it does?'

She rubbed her forehead dazedly. 'After you left the laboratory,' she whispered. 'It was terrifying! I saw myself, in the future, screaming! And the fear in the image entered into me. I knew I was seeing something that was bound to happen! I felt, too, that

I might have done something terrible just before I screamed.'

Bentick frowned. His mind was troubled by her words, as well as thoughts of Dale. He did not now trust the scientist as he might have done earlier. Nargan had been down to the laboratory, and Dale had already disclosed his hate of the man. There was disaster in the not-too-distant future, thought Bentick grimly.

'The Telecopter is certainly an evil invention,' he said. 'It throws out emanations of a similar character to the scenes it shows. For instance, when we saw that age-old conspiracy, I felt as if I were actually taking part in it. It felt like the most important thing in my life for the time it lasted.'

'I felt the same,' said Carol. 'More intensely, perhaps. The Telecopter not only shows events that have happened or will happen, but it also brings to life the emotions involved in those events. That's what terrifies me!'

Bentick reached a decision of the utmost gravity. 'Listen, Carol,' he said earnestly, 'I don't think it's safe for you to be involved in this business. Can't you leave here? Is there anywhere else you could go?'

She shook her head. 'I couldn't leave Dale even if I wanted to. He relies on me. If I wasn't here, he'd starve to death. Besides, there's his work. I'm quite a valuable assistant, although I may not appear to be. I couldn't leave — it wouldn't be fair.'

'All right, then. But do this to please me. Nargan will be gone by tomorrow evening. I have a hunch that Dale's in a strange mood on account of his presence, and I can feel there's danger in the air for everyone till that man has left the house. What I want you to do is stay in your room till then. Lock your door and don't leave under any circumstances.' He broke off for an instant. Then: 'I'll feel a lot happier if you do as I ask, Carol. Somehow or other, your safety and my work seem inextricably mixed. They have been ever since I arrived. Will you do as I ask?'

Carol hesitated. There was doubt in her eyes and uncertainty in the way she looked at him, but in the end she nodded quickly. 'Yes . . . yes, I'll do it, but please be careful. The professor has some plan

81

up his sleeve, I'm sure of it! Even if I stay away from him, I feel that his power — or rather the power of the Telecopter — can reach out to wherever I am. It influences my life now that I've seen what it does. And it frightens me so much that I don't seem to have a will of my own.'

There was an anguish in her voice that troubled the agent, but he smiled reassuringly. 'Everything's going to be all right,' he said gently. 'You rely on me to keep Nargan safe till he's finished here, and I'll be relying on you to stay clear of trouble. As for Dale, I'll keep an eye on him as best I can, but he's his own master of course.'

'Yes — that's what worries me! And I'm not even sure that he *is* his own master! I think the Telecopter rules his life now that he's had success with it. It'll kill him in the end!' She turned away, her eyes dark and unreadable.

Bentick made for the door. 'Take it easy,' he advised. 'The Telecopter isn't going to influence *my* life for me!'

'Isn't it?' she breathed. 'I wonder if you're right.'

Bentick left her room and listened till he heard the key turn sharply in the lock. Then he sighed and went downstairs again, deep in thought.

He saw no sign of Professor Dale or Nargan for several hours, but remained in the library, trying to concentrate on a book and failing miserably. Darkness had fallen by the time Nargan summoned him for food. The man was in a filthy temper, and obviously suffering from a half-concealed fear that plagued him remorselessly. Bentick succeeded in escaping with little more than a few words of abuse after taking a meal to the diplomat's room; then he was once more on his own. There was still no sign of the professor, and he thought it wise not to seek him out. If he was down in the vaults, he would not welcome a visitor.

Bentick dozed in an armchair, mentally tired and less alert than he should have been. When he woke he did so with a guilty start, to find it was well past midnight. The house was dark and silent. He had left a light on in the library, but someone had turned it out as he slept. Cursing himself for a negligent fool, he felt his way across the room and switched on the light again, staring round as if expecting to see some intruder, but there was nothing. He listened intently, but no murmur of sound broke the stillness.

Creeping upstairs, he heard heavy snoring from the other side of Nargan's door. The man was as gross in sleep as he was in waking, thought Bentick. Next he listened at Carol's door, but could hear no sound to indicate that she was either asleep or awake.

Going back downstairs to the library, he sat down after helping himself to a drink, and did some thinking. What was Dale doing now? Was he still playing with the Telecopter; delving further and further into the future or the past? Bentick felt so restless that he could no longer contain his curiosity. He simply had to find out what the professor was doing. Dale was an unknown and unpredictable quantity.

Bentick finished his drink, made sure his automatic was in his pocket, and then left the library. He suffered from doubts about the wisdom of what he was doing when he reached the kitchen, but something stronger than himself drove him on. The steel door to the vault stood slightly ajar, and the air was filled by the high-pitched hum of the generator. He listened intently, then started through the door and crept towards the steps that led down to Dale's sanctuary.

8

Machine Over Mind

Bentick had a feeling that he was walking into some unknown danger. He hesitated on the steps where the gallery branched away on either side. Gazing down to the floor of the laboratory, he made out Professor Dale bending in front of the Telecopter. The man was completely absorbed; and although most of the lights were turned out, there was a faint glow shining on his face from the unseen screen of the machine. From where Bentick stood the screen was not visible, but it was plain that Dale had the machine working from the intensity of his attitude.

Bentick, a prey to all manner of feelings, started working his way cautiously along one branch of the gallery to bring himself to a position from where he would be able to see the screen himself.

The gallery was high above the floor, and he felt sure the professor would not be able to see him in the dim light. Grasping the butt of his automatic in his pocket, he moved with a stealth that surprised him. There was a sense of secrecy in the atmosphere that gripped him irresistibly. He wished he could break it, but the lure of the Telecopter was too strong.

Reaching a point on the gallery level with the back of Dale, he halted, crouching as if to fend off some unseen peril. He noticed that Dale was stooping forward and staring at the screen with a concentration that was somehow terrifying. The professor manipulated the controls of the Telecopter as Bentick had seen him do before. The screen, visible now to the hidden watcher in the gallery, glowed and flickered eerily as time was thrown across its square opalescent surface.

Bentick saw once more the group of Tudor conspirators. The whole spirit of that clandestine meeting seemed to infuse him as he watched. Then Dale made further adjustments and the scene changed abruptly. Now there were only two figures on the screen. A young man, richly dressed in the clothes of another period, was deep in conversation with an older man. This second figure was bearded, and even from a distance Bentick could read the cunning gleam in his eyes. Yet he was smiling easily enough as he talked with the younger of the two.

Bentick had a sudden forewarning that soon he would witness something of a dreadful nature, but still he could not withdraw his gaze from the distant screen and the dim images that moved across it. The younger of the two figures revealed by the Telecopter was plainly in a state of doubt. Bentick came to the conclusion that the old man was trying to persuade him to do something against his will. Just beyond the reach of his comprehension, Bentick knew that he himself was a part of that scene. The power of the emanations that reached him was enormous, stealing his own will and putting in its place something frightening. He was so absorbed that every other thought was driven from his mind. Dale was forgotten, and Carol became a shadow somewhere in his life, but a shadow that had no substance beyond the fact of its being there.

And then, a moment later, the atmosphere was charged with an evil that was greater than ever. The young man on the screen turned away, a worried expression on his face. His companion smiled faintly as he watched. For an instant the figures were immobile, then the old man moved with a lightning gesture and Bentick was seeing an age-old murder committed. There was a knife in the upraised hand of the young man's companion. It caught a gleam of hidden light as it struck, straight for the young man's unprotected back.

The urge to kill swept over Bentick in a manner that stole his reason. At the identical moment of the murder, his hand withdrew his gun from his pocket. An insane desire to kill seized him in a remorseless grip. Without knowing what he was doing, he levelled the gun at Dale's crouching figure on the floor below where he stood. Subconsciously he realised that the professor was holding something in his hand, upraised in a similar attitude to the old murderer's knife. Bentick realised it was a long-bladed screwdriver.

His finger tightened on the trigger of his gun. He had no will of his own outside the insane desire to kill. The power of the Telecopter was boundless.

But Professor Dale saved his own life. With a supreme effort of will, he rose to his feet just as Bentick was about to fire. Throwing a hand across his eyes to fend off the image on the screen, the scientist turned and reached for the main switches, cutting the screen into jagged streaks of light that danced along harmlessly.

Bentick suddenly found himself on the point of killing a fellow-being for no other reason than that something had urged him to do it. He was shaking and sweating as he leaned against the gallery coping, the gun drooping now in his hand. He felt limp and weak, as if all the strength had been sapped from his being by some terrible force. Curiously, he looked down at Dale, the man whom a few moments before he had been about to kill.

The professor was leaning against the Telecopter with one hand thrown across his forehead. Then he shook himself and turned his head, staring round in the glimmer of a small pilot light that shone from the top of the Telecopter. Bentick drew back among the shadows that covered him. He had no real fear that Dale would see him, but he wanted to make quite sure. The scientist, fully recovered now from the effects of that distant murder scene, was once more absorbed with the controls of the Telecopter.

Bentick wondered what other devilry would be portrayed before his eyes; but he, too, was once again in control of his feelings and emotions. He could analyse now what had happened, and was worried by thoughts of Carol. Had she been there in the laboratory when Dale revealed the murder from the past, the professor would probably have killed her in the fit of frenzy brought on by the invisible but powerful emanations that came from the image. Bentick himself might have killed her. So great had been the urge to kill that it would not have mattered who fell victim to it. He shivered at the notion, but once again his whole attention was drawn to the shimmering screen of the Telecopter.

The professor had flicked back from the past to the present; and even as Bentick stared at the screen, the image changed again to some moment in the near future. This time Bentick saw himself as an image. At first he could not quite make out the emotions that assailed him as he watched. The screen was dim and details hard to distinguish, but he was fully conscious of a growing excitement that came from the machine and entered his mind. It was the kind of excitement that someone might feel who had just either witnessed some dramatic act, or was about to take part in it themselves. And as Bentick analysed that far, he saw that the image on the screen held a gun in its hand. There was a thin wisp of bluish smoke curling up from the black-edged muzzle.

He fought for control over himself as he stared at an event in which he would take part before long. It puzzled and worried him, for he could not decide what that smoking gun might mean. And the look on the face of the image was too shadowed to tell what emotion the figure was experiencing.

Before Bentick could arrive at any definite conclusion, Dale was moving on through time, remorselessly, pausing every now and then on the eerie journey through the image world to watch some tiny fragment of action that he gave Bentick no time to follow closely. Then the screen steadied and the picture was plain. Bentick craned his neck as he leaned over the gallery coping. He was no longer in the grip of fear or evil, but was merely a spectator of things he barely understood. Then he was suddenly alive again as he saw Carol's picture before him. He experienced a certain intangible sadness as he watched her. Not for a moment or two did he realise that her image was crying. There were tears on her face, and her hand was unsteady as it went up to cover her eyes from something not shown on the screen.

Bentick felt a great tenderness flow towards her from himself. At the same time, the back of his own figure came into view on the screen as he walked up to her. Instinctively he stretched out a hand while his image put an arm round her shoulders protectively. As if such comfort were too much for her to bear, she collapsed against him, her face buried on his arm. Bentick watched himself lift her and carry her up the steps without effort. At the top, the two of them disappeared out of range of the Telecopter's eye.

Bentick watched himself and Carol fade from the screen. He would have gone on staring at its blankness for a long time had not Dale switched the machine into deadness. He suddenly discovered that his legs were watery and that he was leaning with his full weight on the gallery coping for support. The strain imposed by those emanations he had experienced was greater than he could have imagined. He saw Professor Dale pass a hand across his face and turn away from the Telecopter.

Bentick wondered whether he would be able to slip out unseen, or whether he would have to wait until Dale finally finished and left the laboratory. If that happened, Bentick knew he might find himself locked in for the remainder of the night. It was not a prospect he relished, for Nargan must still be watched; and if he were missing again when the diplomat wanted him in the morning, there would be the very devil to pay.

It was Dale who solved the problem for him, however. The scientist had never looked at the gallery once during the time that Bentick was up there, but suddenly he spoke, quite steadily. 'I should come down from there if I were you, Bentick. I've known you were here all the time, but you needn't think I resent the intrusion. You're always welcome, my friend! Come on down! We must talk!'

9

Problems of a Secret Agent

Bentick pulled himself together with a start. He looked down into the laboratory in amazement, wondering how in the world Dale had known he was there.

'I saw you come in, young man!' the professor called to him. 'I have sharper eyesight than you think, perhaps, but don't let it bother you. Come on down, I say! This is a friendly meeting.'

Bentick grinned as he moved across the gallery and headed for the stairs. His eyes were drawn first to the Telecopter where it stood in the middle of the floor, a strangely potent machine. He was afraid of what it could do to a person, yet he knew there had been times when it had produced sensations that were far from being evil ones. Then his eyes strayed up to the vaulted roof of the ancient crypt that housed the professor's secrets. It was a queer thought to realise that these hewn stones that formed the roof must have been there for centuries, looking down on the events, grim and gay, that he had seen on the screen of the Telecopter. He thought about the murder he had witnessed, and the conspiracy between those people from another period. There was something awesome about watching the whole string of events across time.

He moved down the broad stone steps cautiously, hardly trusting Professor Dale to accept his presence there. That a man like Dale could happily work away and demonstrate the innermost secrets of his latest invention to an unseen watcher without showing resentment surprised him more than he cared to admit, yet Dale had shown nothing in the way of anger when he had called him down.

'Sorry if I intruded, Professor,' said Bentick with a lopsided smile as he arrived at the foot of the steps. He kept one hand in his pocket, grasping his gun in case of accidents. The professor was more than a little mad, he reflected. He might not be dangerous, but there was always a chance. And Bentick did not like taking chances unless he was fully prepared.

As if reading his thoughts, the professor smiled. His eyes were raking Bentick from head to toe, studying the agent in a curiously analytical manner that made the agent feel like a rare insect on an inspection table or beneath the microscope of science.

Dale gave a brief shrug and indicated the work bench. In front of it were two high stools like those in a cocktail bar. They were dirty and their leather seats were stained by chemicals. 'Sit down, Bentick,' the scientist commanded sharply. 'I want to talk to you.' He paused and laughed harshly. 'At least I can make some use of you now that you've broken all the rules of hospitality by spying on me at night!'

Bentick thought it wise to keep quiet for now and let the professor lead the conversation. He sat down uncomfortably on the nearer of the two stools, still with his gun in his hand and his eyes on Dale's face for signs of hostility. There was hidden danger aplenty in this place, he reflected, but that was something he could not fight till it showed itself plainly.

'Now then,' said Dale portentiously, 'I'm going to tell you things that perhaps no other living man will ever hear. You've seen, because I wanted you to, things on the screen of the Telecopter that have stirred you profoundly. Carol, too, has seen strange events. I haven't seen her since she underwent the experience, and I can only assume that she's hidden herself away because she's afraid. She was certainly a prey to fear of the worst possible kind when she left the laboratory some hours ago.'

The professor stopped and approached Bentick closely before continuing. When he finally spoke again, there was a wild light in his eyes that warned the agent to watch his step. 'And as well as you and Carol, someone else has seen things that are hidden from the rest of the world! I refer, of course, to Nargan, that arch-enemy of all humanity, and Britain in particular.'

Bentick shook his head. 'Be careful, Professor, or you'll say things that you'll regret. Nargan may be an unpleasant person, but it's only in the interests of this country that he's here at this moment. If that wasn't the case, our government wouldn't have arranged this meeting in your house.'

The professor made a sweeping gesture with his arm. 'You're mad to think so!' he snapped irritably. 'I tell you, Nargan is the greatest traitor that anyone could ask to their aid. As for doing business with the man on any terms other than your own, it would be sheer folly! I know what I'm saying, do you understand?'

'I'm sure you do,' said Bentick in an attempt to soothe the scientist, 'but this is out of my hands. Even if Nargan is as traitorous as you say, I'm powerless to prevent this meeting from taking place. The moment our representative arrives in the morning, I'm out of the picture. My remit is just to see that Nargan is safe. I met him on his arrival, and soon I'll see him leave. What happens between those two events is nothing to do with me so long as it doesn't affect my immediate duty.' He broke off, watching Dale with a fixed stare that might have troubled a lesser man. 'But I warn you, Professor, that I shall see my duty through no matter what trickery I come up against. Be careful. You would be most unwise to attempt to alter the plans that have been so carefully laid by those in power.'

Dale grimaced sullenly. For an instant he looked like a spoiled child. 'Those in power, as you call them, are fools! I could alter history if I wanted to! Perhaps I shall. Nargan should die! If I could do it myself, I should be quite prepared to take the consequences — but I don't think I'm destined to be the hand that strikes. Nargan will die, all right; and he'll die down here, in all probability. I've already warned him of his doom, and he's frightened!'

Bentick looked at the professor searchingly. The man was a dangerous fanatic, he decided. 'Just exactly how much of the future do you know? Have you seen Nargan die? If you don't tell me, Dale, I'll have you arrested at once and kept out of trouble till this meeting is over.'

The professor burst out laughing. The

echoes were loud in the vaulted laboratory, as if the past and the future were
joining in his bitter mirth. 'Now you
threaten me!' he jeered. 'My dear young
friend, what happens to Nargan will have
nothing to do with me. His fate is beyond
the control of any of us.'

Bentick stared at him shrewdly. Was
this man playing with him? he wondered.
How much could be believed from what
he was saying? Bentick could not trust his
own judgment because he found himself
up against things he could hardly understand. 'Just how much do you know?' he
demanded again.

Professor Dale only smiled. Then: 'You
mean, do I know for certain that Nargan
will die? No. Whatever events lead up to
the scenes you've witnessed on the
Telecopter screen are foreshadowed to
happen beyond its range. You've seen
Carol's image. You've seen your own,
holding a gun that had just been fired.
Someone will die down here, Bentick. I
hope it will be Nargan, but I can't swear
to it. For all I know, you yourself might
kill the traitorous man. There's violence

in the future — always remember that fact!'

'I see,' said Bentick gravely. 'You're playing with dangerous things, Professor. I'd be happier if you left the Telecopter alone till after Nargan has gone. I've a dreadfully solid sort of hunch that he and that machine of yours are going to be involved in some tragedy.' He shrugged. 'If it wasn't for the fact of my own position here, I wouldn't care a hang what became of Nargan, but circumstances compel me to guard his safety with my own life if necessary. Can I rely on you not to jeopardise the situation?'

Professor Dale smiled in a peculiar manner that gave Bentick more worry than he liked to think about. 'You can rely on me to stand and watch future events shape themselves,' he said. 'They're beyond our control. What's reflected by the cosmic radiation *will* happen; that's all you can rely on, Bentick. Now I suggest you return to the upper part of the house and get some sleep.' He paused. 'Your reserves may well be called upon tomorrow.'

Bentick slid off the leather-seated cocktail stool and hesitated. He would have liked to have said a great deal more to Dale, but something stopped him. In the end he gave a helpless shrug and turned away. Halfway up the steps to the gallery, he paused and looked back at the professor. He was standing with his feet apart, his back resting against the Telecopter housing, his eyes returning Bentick's stare. As the agent looked down at him, Dale lifted an arm and waved it slightly. Then he dropped it again wearily, and it hung limp. Bentick wondered when he had slept last.

Without another word, the agent continued his way up the steps and made for the kitchen. His mind was troubled, yet he had so little that was tangible at which to grasp. Dazedly he went upstairs, listened at Nargan's door, and heard the diplomat's heavy snoring. There was no sound from Carol's room.

Bentick drew a chair into the corridor and set it outside Nargan's door. He settled himself down and lit a cigarette, wondering if he would be able to stay awake till the morning. He could not trust himself to sleep again; there were too many shadows of doom around for that. Nargan must be protected — not from outside enemies, but from himself and from Dale. And Bentick had a worrying notion that Dale might be the more dangerous of the two alternatives.

It was almost daybreak.

10

Jagged Nerves

Professor Dale remained in the vaulted laboratory for some time after Bentick had left him. His mind was a sea of various thoughts and ideas, but the one central theme was Nargan and what best to do about him. Dale realised that unless he were very clever, Bentick would prevent him taking action against the foreign visitor he hated so much. And he knew in his heart that he *must* take action. Nargan would have to die before the day was out — and, if possible, before he could do more harm to the interests of Britain.

The professor was certain that Nargan was a menace to the country. He himself had no faith in the people in power, or at any rate not in this thing they were doing by meeting Nargan for an exchange of information. To let the man get away with anything was quite unthinkable — Dale saw it as clearly as a beacon light in his brain; but as yet he could not link up what he felt with a means of achieving his ends. No doubt that would come in time, but the trouble was that time was short. And there was Bentick to contend with as well.

The agent, decided the scientist, was clever enough to pull some trick to wreck his plans. He could not afford to let that happen. But at the same time, he could take no action to stop him. Furthermore, if Nargan died, then it must look as if the professor had had nothing to do with it. He realised that if he killed the diplomat outright with his own hand, then his working days as a scientist would be numbered. And the passion for discovery inside him ruled out such an awful possibility.

With a weary sigh, he turned off the lights in the laboratory and mounted the steps to the kitchen. He had not slept for a considerable time, yet even now he could not afford to do so. What with the success of the Telecopter and the shadow of Nargan's doom hovering at the back of his mind, he was restless and could find no peace. Getting himself something to eat in a picnic fashion in the big kitchen, he stood there with a frown on his face and worried thoughts in his brain.

He went along to the dark library and sank into a chair near the window, finishing a sandwich without tasting it. He had switched on a reading lamp at his elbow and poured himself a drink from the cut-glass decanter. For the first time in hours, he began to feel relaxation flooding through him. But he could not sleep. He thought of Bentick and Nargan and Carol, somewhere upstairs in their rooms. He wondered what thoughts were going through their minds in the darkness that came before dawn. A queer sense of foreboding filled him. The Telecopter had told of violence in the future, but what that violence would be, or how it would come about, he had no idea. That had been hidden; and until he perfected the machine so that its range of vision was widened, he could not know more.

If only there were more time, he told

himself; time to plan and know what would happen exactly before it took place. But it would be many weeks, or even months, before the Telecopter could do all the things he wanted it to do, and during that period Nargan and others like him would be bringing Britain to her knees.

Professor Dale finally rose to his feet as the first streaks of light from the rising sun were seeping in at the window and spreading across the bleak and lonely moor outside. He went upstairs on silent feet, without knowing what took him there. Outside Nargan's room he found Bentick, sound asleep in a chair that barred his way. He could hear the diplomat's gross snores from the other side of the door. He knew without trying it that the door would be locked; that was inevitable. Nargan's fear had been great, and the man was craven enough to think that hiding behind a locked door might save him from the doom that Dale had threatened him with. The professor laughed thinly. There was destiny in the sound.

He stood in the corridor looking at Bentick. The agent was still sleeping, head drooping to one side and one arm slack as it hung over the edge of the chair. The scientist reached out and shook him into wakefulness.

Bentick started violently, opening his eyes and staring round in alarm, hand flashing to his pocket for the feel of his gun.

Dale chuckled. 'You should've learned not to sleep on duty!' he said. 'Suppose I'd been an assassin? What chance would Nargan have stood, eh? You're lucky I'm not that kind of man.'

Bentick rubbed his chin. Fully awake now, he began to wonder whether Dale were toying with him or not. The professor was a cagey person, difficult to deal with unless one knew him well. 'A man has to sleep sometimes,' he said defensively. 'There's little danger to Nargan anyway — except from things we can't understand.'

'Come down and have some breakfast,' said Dale with a friendly smile. 'If you don't have it now while your charge is asleep, he won't give you any peace later.'

Bentick watched him curiously. 'Maybe you're a human being after all. Though I find it hard to believe at times.'

Dale gave a lift of his shoulders, then turned and jerked his head at the door of Carol's room. 'Is she inside? She ought to be up and about by now. We need food, and I need her assistance this morning in the lab.'

Bentick hesitated fractionally. Then: 'She wasn't feeling too good last night. Maybe she's taking a day off, Professor. Better not disturb her. She's labouring under a severe strain of some sort. Perhaps you know the cause yourself.'

The professor did not answer, but walked to Carol's door and knocked on it loudly.

'Who's there?' came her faint answer through the panel. 'You can't come in, whoever you are.'

Dale chuckled again. 'I don't want to, my dear. Are you getting up? It's late, and Bentick and I want our breakfast. So will your friend down the corridor before long, when he wakes up.'

'Go away,' she said in a stifled voice. 'I don't feel well enough to get up this morning. I'm sorry, but you'll have to look after yourselves today.'

She did not sound very sure of herself, thought Bentick grimly. She was still very much afraid, that was obvious, and it was plain as well that Dale was the cause of her fear. Dale and his Telecopter.

The scientist shrugged and started down the corridor. His back had a disapproving look about it; a certain stiffness in bearing that was foreign to his movements.

Bentick consoled himself with the thought that Carol was apparently determined to do as he had suggested and remain in her room till Nargan had left the house. He was glad of that, but wished he could have helped her in a more tangible fashion. Perhaps he'd be able to later on.

After giving the professor time to get down the stairs and disappear from view, Bentick glanced at Nargan's door, gave a sigh of disgust, and followed the scientist to the ground floor of the house. As he reached the big hall, he heard a clang as Dale closed the steel door in the kitchen. Whether Dale had gone below again or not, Bentick did not bother to find out. He was too worried by other things to care at the moment.

Sunlight was streaming in through the tall windows in a warming flood of brilliance. Bentick wished he could have enjoyed it more fully, but his mind gave him little rest from the various problems that faced him. At noon, Britain's representative would arrive at the house, and the meeting and discussion between him and Nargan would take place. What the outcome would be was no concern of Bentick's, but he hoped it would be for the good of Britain, though Dale seemed convinced that the opposite would be the case.

He scratched his chin, not sure whether he wanted a meal or not. In the end he decided that he must have something. And Carol, too, ought to eat. The professor had to be looked after as well, though Bentick didn't worry a lot on that score. And of course there was Nargan, too.

It did not take him very long to find his way round the kitchen and start on his self-imposed duties as servant to the remainder of the people in residence. He made up two trays of food and coffee, one for Carol and the other for Nargan. On the kitchen table he left a place laid for Dale and a note to say there was food in the oven. Then he carried Carol's tray up the stairs and tapped on her door.

'Who is it?' she called uncertainly.

'Bentick. I've brought you some breakfast. Shall I leave it outside the door?'

'Hold on. I'll let you in, in a moment.'

Bentick waited. There was movement in the room, and then Carol turned the key in the lock and opened the door a few inches. She darted a glance up and down the corridor before meeting Bentick's eyes. She was fully dressed, her face was pale, and she looked as if she hadn't slept for long in the night. 'You're very kind,' she said uneasily. 'Bring it in, will you? It's good to see someone reliable again. I've been frightened and so terribly worried all night. Now it isn't so bad.'

Bentick grinned reassuringly and strode

into the room as she stood aside. He put her tray down on the dressing table and turned to face her. She was smiling faintly now. 'Everything's better in daylight with the sun out,' he said. 'You needn't be afraid. If you do as I say and remain in here, you'll come to no harm. Take no notice of Dale; he's a bit on the selfish side, I think. Stick to your story of being ill.'

A shadow crossed her face as he finished speaking. 'Coffee?' she asked hesitantly. 'There's plenty here for both of us.'

Bentick shot her a sideways glance. 'Maybe I'd better not stop,' he said. 'Nargan may wake up at any minute, and then he'll want me for sure. I know his sort. He'll keep me kicking my heels around whether there's any need to or not!'

She shook her head. 'You'll hear him from this room,' she said. 'Please sit down.'

Bentick gave up resisting. He wanted to talk to Carol in any event, but had not wished to force himself on her. There was a jagged edge to her nerves, he could sense it plainly, and his own were none too good at the moment. What Professor Dale's were like he didn't know, but the man didn't seem to have a great many. As for Nargan, the diplomat had been extremely shaken the last time Bentick saw him. A thoroughly disturbed and disturbing household.

'Have you seen the professor again since last night?' Carol asked.

'For a short while,' answered Bentick. He did not want to tell her about his visit to the laboratory in the dark hours; there were things connected with it that were better left unsaid. Later on, perhaps, when matters were straightened out and the unknown or half-known future was clear, he might find the courage to tell her what a strange and terrifying effect Dale's Telecopter had had on his will. But now was certainly not an opportune moment.

'I've left the professor some food ready to eat,' he said. 'There's nothing for you to worry about. Just take it easy.'

She sipped her coffee. 'I wish I could say the same,' she answered wryly. 'I don't quite know exactly what worries me, but there's something at the back of my mind that makes me feel as if I'm no longer my own master. Some influence — left over from the Telecopter, maybe.'

'It'll disappear if you keep away from that screen,' Bentick told her. He was not quite as positive as he sounded, for he, too, felt that nebulous, instinctive lack of willpower. It ate at his nerves and made him feel that if at any given moment something urged him to do a thing against his better judgment, he would do it irresponsibly, regretting it later.

'I wonder if you're right,' said Carol gloomily. 'I wish I could feel as certain as you.'

Bentick forced himself to sound natural when he answered. 'I wasn't so certain myself last night. I think the darkness and the atmosphere in the laboratory worked a kind of spell. It's broken now, thank heavens, but I didn't like it any more than you did while it lasted. Try to forget what's happened.' He watched her eyes as he talked, hoping to see a return of some calm when she heard his words. It flickered there for a moment, but was shadowed again. Then she gave a shaky laugh.

'Nerves, I suppose!' she said. Her voice sounded false.

Bentick might have said more in his efforts to reassure her, but at that moment they both heard Nargan's loud and ill-mannered summons from his room down the corridor. Bentick pulled a rueful face and rose to his feet. 'I'll see you later,' he said, making for the door. 'Don't leave the room, Carol. And don't be afraid. The Telecopter can't hurt you if you stay away from it. Remember that!'

'I'll try.'

Then Bentick was gone, and Carol was alone with her thoughts and fears and that strangely potent influence that haunted her.

11

Nargan is Troubled

Bentick found the diplomat standing in the open doorway of his room. The man's sallow face was flushed and ugly. He held an automatic pistol in one hand and was shaking his other fist at Bentick as the agent reached him.

'What kind of a bodyguard do you think you are?' raved Nargan. 'When I want you, you're always somewhere else! Now I see you coming from the woman's room! This is too much! I've killed men before, and could do the same to you with the greatest ease were you worth a bullet!'

Bentick halted and stared at him with a coldly calculating gaze. 'Are you ready for your breakfast?' he asked at length. 'Maybe you'll feel better when you've got some food inside you. That seems to be your main trouble usually!' He felt like flaying the man.

Nargan almost choked, but controlled himself sufficiently to gulp back an angry retort that rose to his lips. Instead he drew a deep breath and thrust his gun away savagely. 'You're not even fit to serve me!' he snapped. 'But I will eat. Let's go downstairs at once!'

Bentick looked at him shrewdly. 'I thought you wanted your meals in your room. Have you changed your mind?'

'Is it any concern of yours what I choose to do? Yesterday I had a headache. Today I'm feeling fine. Hurry now — I'm hungry!'

Bentick grinned to himself. Nargan was far from fine, he reflected. His hands were shaking even now, and his eyes were never still for more than a second at a time. He, too, was apparently suffering from an attack of nerves; a kind of mental hangover from his experience with the Telecopter. The machine had a wide range of influence, thought Bentick grimly. Aloud he said: 'I'm glad to hear it! I had your meal ready to bring up, but if you'd rather come down, so much the better.'

'We're wasting time,' snapped Nargan, thrusting past him. Bentick followed him down the stairs, fuming all the way. This, he thought, was the queerest, most unpleasant job he had ever been involved in. He had undertaken many others that were far more dangerous, but none with such an ungraspable sense of evil.

Somewhat to Bentick's surprise, and much to his interest, they found Professor Dale sitting at the big kitchen table. The scientist was eating as if he had not seen food for weeks, and Bentick wondered how Carol ever made him have any meals to a routine at all. Probably she didn't.

At sight of Nargan, the professor put his knife and fork down with a double thud on either side of his plate and eyed him narrowly. There was a faintly cynical light in his stare, as if he were probing into Nargan's mind with a microscopic insight that missed very little.

Nargan halted on the threshold of the kitchen and met the professor's gaze. Bentick, close at his heel like a faithful but resentful dog, sensed the battle that was going on wordlessly between these two. Both were strong; but whereas Dale feared nothing, the same could not be said for Nargan.

Dale said: 'So we meet again, my friend!' He smiled. 'Do come in and make yourself welcome. The food is fair, but the service poor. My ward, you understand, is not feeling very well and is confined to her room. You must forgive her.'

Nargan had time during the professor's sarcastic little speech to pull himself together. He seized the tenor of the situation and answered in kind. 'You are most thoughtful, Professor.' There was barely the hint of a sneer in his words, but it was not very far below the surface. 'Naturally,' he continued, 'I'm used to better conditions than are offered here, but there are times when we all have to make allowances, are there not?' He smiled in an oily, fulsome fashion and went towards the table.

Dale watched him closely. 'We certainly do,' he said feelingly. Then he picked up his knife and fork and went on with his meal in silence. Nargan shot him a quizzical glance, but the professor was now entirely absorbed, ignoring the diplomat as if he did not exist.

Bentick, feeling uncomfortable with the heavy atmosphere that surrounded the two men, busied himself and soon had Nargan's breakfast before him. It was a duty that galled him considerably, but under the present circumstances it was unavoidable. His only consolation was that this state of affairs would not be a lengthy one.

After continued silence for several minutes, it was Dale who spoke again. 'I trust you slept well?' he said to Nargan.

The diplomat blinked at him owlishly. He was putting on a stupid act, but it did nothing to fox either Bentick or the professor. 'I always sleep well,' he grunted ungraciously. 'But I must admit I've slept in more comfortable beds than the one I was given.'

Dale let it pass. Then: 'You weren't troubled by evil thoughts or the ghosts of unseen events, then?'

Nargan's eyes flickered as he stared at Dale icily. 'I don't know what you mean. If it's of interest to you, I slept very well. Nothing ever troubles me at night.'

Dale grinned vindictively. 'I hope you'll always be able to say the same!' he retorted. 'Some men aren't as fortunate as you.' He pushed back his plate and sat there smiling in a strangely disarming manner. Then he rose to his feet and hesitated, looking from Nargan to Bentick.

Bentick, leaning against the end of the table with his hands on the edge, grinned boyishly. He still did not trust Professor Dale, but the scientist seemed to be far more human now than on the previous night. Maybe he wasn't so bad outside his laboratory or under the gentle influence of sunshine, he thought. He wished he could say the same for Nargan.

Dale gave a nod, then shook himself. Addressing Bentick, he said: 'Would you be kind enough, young man, to let me know when our second visitor arrives? If it's who I think it is, we're well acquainted. I should like the opportunity of seeing him and having a talk on certain extraneous matters unconnected with his purpose here. You'll find him quite charming, I believe. Please do your best to make things easy for him.'

Bentick nodded. 'Certainly, Professor. I'll pass on your message if I can't let you know directly. You may rely on me.'

Dale grunted. 'It's a good thing I can rely on someone!' he said maliciously. 'Maybe I'm wrong even then.'

Bentick made no reply. He glanced at Nargan and caught the ugly glint in his eyes. The diplomat was going to be awkward, he decided.

Dale walked across to the steel door, disappeared through it, and closed it behind him. Both Nargan and Bentick heard the click of the lock as the key was turned.

Bentick lit a cigarette and drifted over to the window. His thoughts turned to Dale's Telecopter and what its screen had foreshadowed. Why had it shown him in the vaulted laboratory with a smoking gun in his hand? Why should Carol be down there again, prey to fear and in need of comforting? What fiendish events were going to happen in that age-old place below the ground? He could find no answer to the queries that teased his brain, yet he had a hunch that behind it all was the sinister Telecopter itself, a presence of evil that would eventually wreak havoc on everyone in its vicinity.

Nargan finished his meal in something of a hurry. He got up, slapped his stomach resoundingly, and glared at Bentick with a baleful light in his eyes. 'I'm going to my room,' he announced curtly. 'You'll remain nearby, instead of being absent as you were on previous occasions. The moment your country's representative shows up, inform me. That's an order, and I'll brook no disobedience, so do not fail!'

Bentick gave him look for look. 'I'm not in the habit of making mistakes. Is there any other demand you have to make?' He found it extremely difficult to keep the insolent note from his words, but prudence dictated that he must remain on amicable terms — outwardly, at any rate — with Nargan. To rib the man further would only make things more difficult.

The diplomat scowled at him. 'I have no further orders at the moment,' he said at length. 'I'm going upstairs now, but remember what I said.' He turned on his heel and started for the door. Just as he reached, it Professor Dale opened the laboratory door and poked his head round the corner. Nargan halted abruptly, staring at him.

Dale grinned impishly. 'Don't forget what I told you yesterday, Nargan,' he said ponderously. 'The future is dangerous for you. There's violence in the air! Remember that!' Before Nargan could answer, he slammed the door again and disappeared once more.

Bentick looked at the diplomat curiously. He was pale, with an ashy tint to his sallow skin. A livid patch showed on his cheek as he stood there breathing hard, fingers clenching and unclenching spasmodically as fear took a grip on his nerves.

'The professor talks in riddles,' said Bentick with an attempt at lightness.

Nargan controlled himself with an enormous effort. He rounded on the agent like a cornered tiger. 'I'll give him riddles before I'm through in this cursed country!' he snarled. 'He'll regret all his clever talk and the things he produces by trickery! I shall break him completely, I tell you! Wait till I speak to your representative. That will finish this cocksure professor of yours!'

Bentick smiled sourly. 'I wouldn't be too sure of that,' he murmured.

Nargan snorted and marched from the room without another word. Bentick smiled again and watched him leave.

12

Dale and the V.I.P.

After Nargan left the kitchen, Bentick stayed behind for several minutes deep in thought. His chief worry was what would happen when the other half of the conference arrived. Would the V.I.P. who was representing Britain know Nargan for what he was? Had they ever met before? What kind of impact would the diplomat have on the shrewd man of state that would meet him in this lonely house on the Cornish moors? Only time could supply the answers to Bentick's questions.

He toyed with the idea of going down to the laboratory for another talk with Professor Dale. Then he wondered if he should go up and see Carol again; they had not achieved a great deal between them when he'd taken her breakfast up. But what he chose to do in the end was drift along to the library and while away an hour in sitting near the window with the warming sunlight streaming through the casements and spilling on the floor around him. There were many things he could not think about clearly, and one of those was the influence of the Telecopter. He knew it to be an evil thing, but how it could be fought he had no idea. Why did Dale have to go and invent a devil's instrument of that sort? Probing the future was asking for trouble.

The morning passed quietly enough, and Bentick saw no further sign of either Carol or the professor. Nargan kept strictly to himself behind a locked door upstairs. Either he was taking no chances, or his own inmost fear was too great to brave the remainder of the household should he meet them by accident.

At five minutes to midday, Bentick was startled from one of his reveries by the sound of a car coming up the overgrown drive of the house and halting at the front door with a crunch of gravel beneath its tyres. Getting to his feet, he glanced through the library window and saw a sleek-looking car, with a second one in attendance behind bearing the colours of the police department. Even as Bentick watched, doors opened and uniformed men stepped out. An immaculate individual in smart morning clothes alighted from the leading vehicle. He carried a bulging briefcase under one arm and glanced about inquiringly.

One of the police officers started towards the door, but by then Bentick had left the library and was going down the hallway to meet the visitor. He had recognised the man's identity at once, for Victor Barringville was a national figure. It had been through his clever agency that a world war had been averted some ten years previously; and although a comparatively young member of the statesmen, he was acknowledged as being one of the most capable in the country. How he and Nargan would get along was a matter that intrigued Bentick enormously.

The agent reached the front door before anyone outside could knock, opened it and stood aside, smiling pleasantly at Barringville and the tall police officer who accompanied him. Barringville was usually very averse to having an escort, but on this occasion it had apparently been considered essential.

The immaculate statesman surveyed Bentick with eyes that had a humorous twinkle behind them. 'So you're Bentick, are you?' he said as he stepped through the open door. 'I've heard of you. Cain gave me some very good reports on your work. I hope everything's been satisfactory down here?'

Bentick hesitated. 'On the whole, yes,' he answered. 'Though there are one or two matters I'd like to mention to you in private, sir. But come into the library. I'll just inform Nargan that you're here.'

But Barringville stopped him. 'No particular hurry,' he said. 'What is this man like, Bentick? I've never met him before, and the issues are so grave that I'd value an outside opinion on his character before forming my own. At the moment I only have hearsay to go by.'

Bentick was surprised that an eminent man such as Barringville should ask for his opinion. It was disturbing as well as flattering. Should he tell him what he thought? Or should he make some evasion and leave that part of it to Professor Dale?

The statesman read his embarrassment plainly enough. 'Don't be afraid to tell me exactly what you think of him,' he said. 'I'm led to believe that you're a pretty shrewd fellow, and a moment ago you spoke of certain delicate matters that worried you.'

Bentick grinned a trifle sheepishly. 'Well, sir, in that case I'll be quite frank with you. Nargan is one of the most detestable people I've ever run across. But quite apart from a strong personal dislike of him, I don't trust him either. He's what I would call a double dealer. If you won't be offended, I should like to say that I advise the utmost caution in dealing with him.'

Barringville watched him narrowly as he spoke. Then he nodded soberly. 'I was already prepared to do so,' he murmured. 'Thank you, Bentick. You've been most helpful.' He smiled in his usual urbane, charming manner. 'There's nothing quite like someone else's first-hand experience to assist one in basing an opinion.'

Bentick grinned. 'You're very kind, sir. And now, shall I go and tell him you're here? He gave me strict orders to do so the moment you arrived. He isn't enjoying his visit very much, I'm afraid, and is anxious to get this meeting over with so that he can return to his own country. He's a very rude man, and doesn't pull his punches.'

'So I've already gathered,' Barringville said dryly. 'Yes, perhaps you'd better let him know I'm here. But, first of all, where's Professor Dale?'

Bentick rubbed his chin for an instant. 'The last time I saw him, he was going down to his underground lab. He especially asked me to tell him when you came as well. You're a much sought-after man, sir! Whom shall I tell first?' Bentick grinned at the immaculate statesman.

'I know Dale very well indeed. Perhaps it'd be as well to have a word with him before I go into conference with Nargan. It's only fair, considering that this is his house and we're making a convenience of his good-heartedness.'

Bentick nodded quickly. 'If you stay here, sir. I'll go and tell him you'd like a word with him.'

Barringville sat himself down in Bentick's vacated chair and stretched his long legs out straight in front of his lean, muscular body. His hands were thin but remarkably capable-looking. His face was handsome, yet showed traces of the strain under which he often worked. There was also a hint of the iron will inside him that showed in his eyes and the line of his jaw. Barringville was an ideal man to handle a deal with Nargan. He was an ideal man to handle any deal, come to that.

Bentick went through to the kitchen as quickly as he could; he did not want Nargan to discover he was telling the professor of Barringville's arrival first. There was a chance that the diplomat might already have heard the two cars draw up, of course, but if so he would come downstairs without being fetched.

In the kitchen Bentick found that the steel door to the laboratory steps was locked. He looked round and discovered a small bell push beside the framework.

Putting his thumb on the button, he pressed it firmly. The period of waiting seemed interminable, but at long last the door opened soundlessly and Professor Dale stood before him, an inquiring look on his face and a long-bladed screwdriver in one hand.

'Oh, excuse me, Professor,' Bentick began, 'but I thought you'd like to know that Barringville has arrived. You did ask me to let you know at once, if you remember.'

The professor's face altered in some subtle fashion that was hard to describe. Then he beamed at Bentick. 'Ah yes, of course!' he said hurriedly. 'I was busy, but it doesn't matter in the least. Where is he? Have you made him comfortable?'

'As well as I could. He's in the library now. He said he'd like a word with you before he sees Nargan. Will you come along, or shall I tell him to join you in the lab?'

Dale hesitated for a fraction of a second, then made up his mind. Thrusting the screwdriver into the top pocket of his stained overalls, he pushed past the agent and hastened from the kitchen, leaving the steel door open and the faint but insistent hum of the generator whining through the air.

Bentick glanced through the door at the passage beyond. He wondered if the professor had left the Telecopter in action, and what he would see if he broke all the rules and went down to take a look. He might have risked it had not a sudden noise erupted from somewhere upstairs. Bentick sighed as he recognised the bull-like roar of an infuriated Nargan on the rampage. Quickly drawing the steel door to, he hurried from the kitchen and went to the foot of the stairs.

The diplomat was standing at the top, quivering with mingled rage and nerves. At the sight of Bentick, he stopped his bellowing and glared at him savagely. 'Why was I not informed that your upstart politician was here?' he demanded.

Bentick stole a glance at the door of the library and saw that it was closed. Dale and Barringville must have heard Nargan shouting. They must have been able to hear what he had just said, too, but they apparently meant to remain out of sight till Barringville was ready to receive him. Bentick caught the eye of the uniformed police officer standing guard at the front door of the house. The officer gave a shrug and raised his eyebrows slightly. Bentick gave him a fleeting wink.

'Our visitor's refreshing himself after the journey,' Bentick said, turning his attention to Nargan again.

The diplomat snarled something incomprehensible and tramped away, making for his own room again. '*He* shall wait for *me* in that case!' he snapped as he disappeared. 'Call me in an hour's time!'

Bentick grinned and spread his hands helplessly. He felt he was not shining very brightly in his handling of this particular affair. The only consolation was that in all probability, an hour's interval would please Barringville well enough, for it would give him a chance to talk with Dale and form his own ideas.

Bentick decided to have a word with the statesman on the subject of Dale and the Telecopter. He felt that someone other than those in the immediate household ought to know about it. If that someone was anyone as reliable as Barringville, there could be no harm in talking about it. In any event, he guessed that Dale would probably have told the great man about his latest invention. But what Barringville would not be aware of was the queer and frightening effect the machine could have on those who watched its screen.

Standing outside the library door, Bentick found that it was not quite closed, as he had at first imagined. He could hear the scientist and the statesman talking together. Barringville was asking how Dale was progressing with his work.

'My dear fellow,' Dale answered, 'I've recently made the greatest discovery of my career. Using cosmic radiation and the echoes of events in the space-time continuum, I've created a machine that can televise things that have happened or will happen in the future. Given time, there's no limit to the far-reaching results this apparatus will achieve. I shall have pleasure in giving you a personal demonstration before you leave here.'

Barringville was obviously intrigued. Dale went on: 'I've already foreseen some kind of violence taking place down there. I hope it may lead to the death of Nargan, for the man's a traitor to everyone. If you're wise, you'll give him no information whatever, as you had planned to do.'

Bentick heard a stiffness in Barringville's voice. 'Professor,' he said, 'that's a matter which rests entirely with me. You can rely on my not making any mistakes in this business. Since the very safety of the world may depend on this meeting, I shall give it due thought and consideration. I must ask you not to interfere in any way; and as for Nargan dying in this house, the very idea of his death or injury appals me. That's all I can say.'

13

Secret Conference

Bentick smiled faintly to himself as he stood outside the door and listened to Barringville's words. That, he reflected, should tell the professor to watch his step! But Dale was a determined man. His work itself was a monument to perseverance, for of its very quality it demanded the utmost concentration and patience.

Bentick heard him laugh gently, then: 'You sound quite pompous, Barringville! That's all you can say, is it? Let me warn you that Nargan isn't the straight-dealing person you believe him to be. I've seen into the future, my friend, and I can also sense his treachery. The others will probably tell you the same. Bentick, for instance, has had quite a lot to do with him. He doesn't like him any more than I do, and I doubt if he trusts him as far.' Again he laughed. 'In fact, I have an idea that Bentick doesn't trust *me* very much!'

'Bentick is a shrewd fellow,' said Barringville. 'I have a lot of faith in him, Dale, but I don't think he'd make a mistake like that. Now, I'm afraid I can't spare any more time for this interesting discussion. Nargan will be growing restless and impatient, and I have no doubt that in such a mood he'll be even more difficult to deal with. We shall see!'

Bentick heard a chair being pushed back, and he knocked on the door before Barringville could reach it. 'You heard Nargan yelling a little while ago, sir?' he asked as the statesman appeared.

'Yes,' Barringville admitted ruefully. 'It seems he's just as rude as you told me he was! But that can't be helped. What did he have to say?' He paused. 'I missed the last few remarks he made as he left.'

'They weren't important. He told me to call him in an hour. He said he'd be ready to see you then, the idea being to make you wait for him instead of the other way around. A most offensive person.'

Barringville's mouth contracted slightly. 'Yes,' he agreed, 'I'm beginning to think so myself, after what I've heard and been told. But there's no hurry as far as I'm concerned, and by the time he's ready he'll probably be in a better temper.' He gave the agent a smile.

The professor came out of the library at that moment and shot a glance at Bentick. There was some meaning behind it, but the agent could not put his finger on it. He felt that Dale was playing some cagey kind of game that was all his own, and the notion worried him a great deal.

Both he and Barringville watched the figure of Dale disappear in the direction of the kitchen and his underground laboratory. The statesman frowned in a puzzled fashion. 'A strange man,' he murmured, 'but remarkably clever.'

'Rather too clever for my liking,' Bentick said with a nod. 'I hope I'm not treading on anyone's toes, sir, but I think Dale's more than a little mad, and he's playing with things that are far more dangerous than explosives. I don't know how much he told you about the Telecopter, but when you see it you'll understand.'

Barringville eyed him inquiringly. 'What exactly do you mean by that?' he asked quietly.

'There's something uncanny about its influence. It not only does what the professor claims, but it destroys a person's willpower as well. Such a thing can't be good, can it?'

Barringville shifted his gaze. 'I can't form an opinion yet,' he replied evasively. 'Dale and I have been friends for many years. I know he's eccentric, of course, but it's hard to say whether he's actually mad or not. A small thing might make him so, and genius and madness are close together; but I don't want to say any more.'

'Of course not, sir. It was only an idea I had. But this Telecopter has already caused some problems.'

'Has it indeed? In what way, Bentick?'

'Carol Collins, the professor's ward, felt its aura so strongly that her nerves failed her. I've advised her to remain in her room till Nargan's gone. What with him and the Telecopter, I thought it best to keep her clear of things.'

The statesman frowned. 'You raise my

interest in this machine the more I hear about it,' he mused. 'I shall certainly persuade Dale to give me a demonstration as soon as possible. He already said he would.'

Bentick gave him a doubtful look. 'You're as curious as I was at first, sir. I hope you don't feel as scared of the wretched thing as I did afterwards!'

Barringville grinned at him. 'Maybe I shall, maybe I shall. Now, perhaps Nargan will be prepared to receive me,' he added a little sarcastically. 'Will you be good enough to convey my respects to the gentleman?'

'With pleasure, sir!' Bentick answered with a chuckle.

'I'll wait in the library,' the statesman called as Bentick turned away. 'Don't let anyone disturb us, there's a good man. I've already given the police officer instructions to post a guard on the door, but he isn't going to do it till Nargan joins me.'

'Right!' answered Bentick briefly. 'I'll be around if you want me, sir.'

Halfway up the stairs he glanced back, seeing the tall statesman standing by the library door watching him with a faint smile on his lips. Bentick continued on his way up the stairs.

He knocked on Nargan's door and waited. There was an appreciable interval before the diplomat answered, and then Bentick heard the key grate harshly as it was turned. The two of them stood for a moment, staring at each other in silence.

Finally Bentick said: 'Are you ready for the conference? Our man's waiting in the library. No one will disturb you while you talk.'

Nargan showed his teeth in a wolfish grin. 'He can wait a little longer!' he snapped. 'Then I shall take great pleasure in meeting him and showing him that I'm not a man to trifle with! Nor is my country a puny state such as yours! Britain must come to heel, as other nations have in the past — and I, Nargan, shall ensure that she does!'

Bentick compressed his lips. 'I trust you'll have no further complaints to make when you achieve your object,' he said tightly. 'This is a matter of lasting peace for the world. My country will do all it can to preserve it. Any move in the opposite direction will be your doing, Nargan, not ours. I'll leave you to make your own way down to the library.'

He left Nargan standing where he was, because he knew that if he remained himself he would say things that Barringville would not thank him for. Nargan returned into his room and slammed the door behind him.

Bentick suddenly felt a strong urge to go down to the laboratory; it was as if some power beyond his control were calling to him. Only with the greatest difficulty did he succeed in fighting the instinctive prompting that made him turn his eyes in the direction of the kitchen as he reached the hall. 'Curse this scientific magic!' he muttered. 'Dale and his inventions will be the death of someone before he's through.' Then he caught himself. There was a certain prophetic ring about those words that worried him.

Going to the library instead of the kitchen, he told Barringville that Nargan would be down in his own good time. The statesman frowned, but there was nothing that either of them could do to hurry things along. 'All right, Bentick, and thank you for all you've done since I got here,' said Barringville. 'Don't let things worry you. It doesn't help in the least, and I'm gradually getting a feel for the atmosphere in this house. It isn't particularly pleasant, I agree, but I've known worse.'

'Wait till the professor's through with the Telecopter,' answered Bentick darkly. 'There aren't many worse things than that, I assure you!'

Barringville only smiled. Bentick realised he had no right to speak to the great man in the way he'd been doing, and beat a hasty retreat. Some prompting urged him to make for the kitchen again, but before he had passed the foot of the stairway Nargan came down slowly and carefully. He ignored Bentick as if he did not exist, going straight to the library door and throwing it open without the courtesy of a knock.

Bentick hesitated, watching as a police officer from outside the front door appeared and went silently to stand with his back to the library entrance. They eyed each other and nodded, then Bentick turned away again, wondering how Barringville and Nargan were hitting it off at this, their first and probably last meeting.

The urge to go to the kitchen came again, but this time Bentick was ready for it and purposefully altered his direction towards the stairs. He wanted to find out how Carol was feeling, and now seemed as good an opportunity as any he was likely to get before he left the house.

Tapping her door panel lightly, he waited, listening with his head to one side. She wasted little time in answering his knock, and he was glad to see that she looked less strained than she had done previously. 'Come in,' she invited, standing aside as he hesitated. 'What news have you got? I heard cars pull up. Is it your statesman here to meet with Nargan?'

Bentick nodded, stepped into the sun-lit room and glanced round. He remembered the feeling of tenderness he had experienced when he beheld himself on the Telecopter screen comforting

Carol at some moment in the future. There was a queer kind of torment in the memory. Bentick crushed it down and tried to sound matter-of-fact.

'Yes,' he answered. 'Our man and Nargan are now holding their meeting. I'm free of my duties for a short time, and then I hope I'll be shot of Nargan for good.'

'Where's the professor?' asked Carol tensely. 'I've a feeling he's got the Telecopter working again. Can you sense it in the atmosphere, Bentick? It's odd, but the idea's so strong that I can't get it out of my head. Queer, isn't it?' She watched him anxiously, as if she expected him to laugh at her.

He frowned. 'Yes, it's queer,' he admitted. 'I can feel it myself, but you mustn't let it disturb you. Barringville, the man who's come to meet with Nargan, is going to see the Telecopter later on. If he feels as we do about what its possibilities are, I should think he'd take steps to caution the professor. That machine could never bring good to humanity, I'm sure of it!'

'You've seen it again, haven't you?'

Carol said accusingly. 'I know you have, so don't deny it. You must've gone down to the lab last night after I'd gone to my room and locked myself in. What did you see on that screen? You've got to tell me! I know there's danger ahead. I'm too sensitive not to realise it.'

Bentick swallowed painfully. How could he tell her what he'd seen? And how could he be sure that she wouldn't fall prey to that influence and leave her room? He knew she would eventually enter the vaulted laboratory again — the foreshadowed events made that as certain as anything ever could be. The idea worried him more and more.

'If there's danger, it doesn't concern you,' he said. 'And don't worry — this will all come right in the end.'

She met his gaze steadily. 'I hope so,' she said.

14

Invitation to a Vault

'I'm sure of it,' went on Bentick quickly, taking advantage of the note of uncertainty in her voice. 'If there's danger in the future, it doesn't concern you.'

'Yet I can't bring myself to feel as certain of that as you are,' she said quietly. 'There are so many shadows at the back of my mind. I'm moving through a fog that began in the laboratory, but now it's stretched and stretched till it reaches me even here.' Her tone rose slightly as she spoke, and the growing strain was visible on her face.

'Steady on,' said Bentick firmly. 'Just leave everything to me and stay in here, whatever happens. It won't be for very much longer, because I've got a hunch that anything that's going to happen will happen while Nargan is still in this house. And he's leaving tonight, don't forget.'

Carol looked at him steadily. She seemed to be surer of herself now, but when she spoke again there was a queer kind of chill in her words. 'I wonder if you're right,' she said. 'I wonder if he *will* leave.'

'For heavens' sake, don't say things like that,' Bentick grunted.

'Sorry,' she said with a faint smile. 'Maybe you'd better go now. It's helped a lot to talk to you, Bentick. You're a pretty good leaning post, you know.'

He laughed unsteadily. 'Come to that, you aren't so bad yourself,' he said softly. 'I can't deny that I find talking to you a very great help indeed. Now, I'll leave you in peace and get downstairs again to wait for the others to finish their conference. By then I suppose we'll have the professor on the scene again.' He frowned. 'It's him I'm worried about as much as anyone, you know. He's the cause of all the trouble, really. But Barringville seems to think he's all right — if a little eccentric.'

Carol turned away and walked to the window, standing before it and staring out at the lonely sweep of moorland beyond. The thoughts in her brain brought little comfort. 'I'll stay where I am,' she said over her shoulder. 'You needn't be afraid that I won't. I'll lock the door behind you.'

Bentick hesitated, shifting from one foot to the other. 'I'd feel happier if you let me lock it on the outside, but I know it's too much to ask. You've got a will of your own in spite of the Telecopter, Carol, so I won't insult it.' He opened the door and waited for a moment.

She came across the room and put a hand on his arm. 'Thank you,' she said. 'I'll see you before you go, won't I?'

He gave her a sudden grin. 'I shouldn't be at all surprised! I'll be around, don't worry.'

Outside in the corridor, Bentick paused as the door closed behind him. His ears picked up the click of the lock and he felt relieved. Carol was going to be all right; of course she was. He knew that from what the Telecopter had shown. But the unknown intermediate events still troubled his mind.

He went down the stairs to the hall.

The police officer was still standing with his back to the door of the library. They grinned and nodded to each other. Bentick lit a cigarette and lingered, uncertain what to do next. The urge to discover what Professor Dale was up to grew with every moment he stayed in the hall. He went along to the kitchen and looked around, but there was no one there, and the steel door to the laboratory was shut. He walked slowly towards it and turned the handle. Something stronger than himself made him do it.

The door was locked and refused to move when he thrust his shoulder against its cold surface. Putting his ear close to the steel, he could just make out the hum of the generators down below. So Dale was probably using the Telecopter, he thought. He wondered what shadows and figures were crossing and re-crossing that devilish screen.

With marked reluctance, he turned away and rummaged in one of the kitchen cupboards for something to drink. He found a bottle and glass and helped himself to some Scotch. Every now and again his eyes strayed to the laboratory door. It was as if there were a powerful magnet in place behind its blankness that drew him remorselessly. Bentick had never considered himself a sensitive person, but he was certainly sensitive to the emanations of the Telecopter. He shivered when he remembered how strong the influence had been when he'd witnessed the murder scene the previous evening.

The machine was destructive, bringing to life the dreadful emotions that were connected with the events it showed. But then he recalled that those emotions were not always negative. He remembered the scene in which he'd comforted Carol; it brought steadiness to the doubts inside him. Perhaps the Telecopter was not entirely bad; perhaps there were ways in which it could work some good. He wished it could solve all the problems that confronted the troubled world, but he doubted if anything created by humankind could do that.

Finishing his drink and staring at the empty glass with a sour grimace, Bentick suddenly shook the depression from his shoulders and walked from the kitchen with a new determination. He glanced at the policeman in the hallway. The man shook his head and jerked a thumb in the direction of the library door at his back. 'Still at it!' he said. 'I'm glad I'm not mixed up in this! Looks as if it'll go on for a long time yet.'

Bentick nodded. He thought so too. Barringville was not a man to give any points away till he was sure he was getting full value in return. 'I'll be pleased when Nargan goes,' he said. 'He's my particular pigeon, and a pretty unpleasant bird at that!'

The officer grinned and nodded. 'So I should think! Still, it takes all kinds, don't it? This is a rum affair taken all round. Can't say I fancy it much, do you? Queer kind of house as well. Something odd about the atmosphere, if you know what I mean.' He looked at Bentick sideways as he spoke.

Bentick reflected that apparently he was not the only one to fall victim to the Telecopter's emanations. Others beside himself were sensitive to the waves and echoes it sent out invisibly. 'Maybe you're right,' he grunted. 'The trouble is that we're all getting jittery, which is quite absurd.'

'You should know!' said the officer. 'I've only been here long enough to get a feeling about it. That's bad enough.'

Bentick made no reply. He was worried and couldn't hide the fact, but he did not wish to give any information away to a stranger. He frowned, shrugged, and turned on his heel, making for one of the other vacant rooms on the ground floor. From the look of its furniture it was nominally a dining room, he guessed, but since he and Nargan had been in the house they had only sat down at the table once, and that on arrival. Now it provided a haven for the agent where he could be alone with his thoughts.

Eventually his reverie was interrupted by the sound of the police officer's voice in the hall outside. 'Sorry, sir,' he was saying, 'but you can't go in there. Conference in progress. Very important that the gentlemen aren't disturbed.'

Professor Dale's querulous voice came

after a moment's pause. 'But that's non-sense! I have a right to enter rooms in my own house, haven't I?'

'Sorry, sir,' repeated the policeman stubbornly. 'I've got my orders, and you'll have to wait. No offence meant, of course, but there's nothing else for it.'

Dale grunted. Bentick, in the dining room, sighed and rose to his feet. He supposed that he'd better go out and take the professor away before the policeman had to be more emphatic. What the professor wanted in there Bentick did not know, but it was quite out of the question to let him in.

He strolled into the hall and smiled, seeing Dale in front of the officer with a sulky look on his face. 'Why hello, Professor. What's the trouble?'

Dale faced him with an exasperated look in his eyes. 'I want a word with Barringville, that's all,' he said. 'It's important!'

Bentick spread his hands. 'It couldn't be more so than what's going on in there right now. I'm afraid you'll have to be patient. Come and wait in the dining room with me till they're through. We've plenty to talk about between us. I'd like to know more about your work — about the Telecopter, for instance.' He watched Dale as he talked, anxious to strike the right note with the scientist and draw him away from further embarrassment.

Dale smiled in a cunning fashion. 'You are clever, young man!' he said. 'Yes, I know exactly how your mind is working! And you chose a very good subject to attract my attention. Very well, then, I'll wait till Barringville is free, though Nargan is taking up a great deal of valuable time.'

Bentick covered a weary sigh. 'I'm sure he'll be only too delighted to see you presently, Professor. In the meantime, why don't you come into the dining room with me and take it easy for a while?'

'Neatly handled, Bentick!' Dale grinned approvingly.

Bentick flushed. He had not been very clever after all; but though the professor could apparently see through him as plainly as a sheet of glass, he was ready enough to be drawn away from his original intention.

Dale took Bentick by the arm and steered him back into the dining room whence he had come. Bentick felt rather like a small boy.

'Now then, the Telecopter!' whispered the scientist in a tone of conspiracy. 'I've been using it again, my boy!'

'So I guessed. I can feel when that machine is working.'

Dale eyed him keenly. 'It has a strong influence, does it not? I've suffered all manner of emotions down there since you watched from the gallery. The Telecopter is growing to be something of a drug without which I cannot exist. There's a power in it, Bentick! A power for good as well as evil, let me add! And I think that before long some good *will* come from it.'

Bentick gave him a suspicious glance. 'I certainly hope so!' he muttered. 'But I can't help feeling that you're wrong. Nothing really and truly good could come from *that* source!'

Dale grinned, showing his teeth almost savagely. 'What a doubter you are!' he scolded. 'Science and everything connected with it is good. Even the devastation caused

161

by science is good if it furthers human-kind's knowledge to any degree. Look what miracles of progress arose from the harnessing of atomic power after its initial use as a weapon of destruction! Now we're the masters of it, though at first it brought misery and death to thousands. Since those days, half our needs are catered for by the harnessed atom and the forces within it. You can't deny that, now, can you?'

Bentick hesitated. 'No, I suppose I can't,' he admitted. 'But I still think it's dangerous for humans to seek foreknowledge of events that are yet to come.'

Dale only laughed; then he started striding up and down the room impatiently, hands linked behind his back and head thrust forward hawkishly. 'You don't understand the mind of a scientist!' he snapped. 'And why should I attempt to explain such a thing to one as ignorant as you? It's sufficient, I think, to tell you that time will prove me to be correct, be sure of that. Until it does, I must ask you to agree with me, or keep quiet altogether.' He rounded on Bentick as he finished, glaring at him balefully.

The agent smiled. 'That's all right by me, Professor,' he said. Privately he considered the man to be a little more unbalanced than before, but it wouldn't do to say so.

'Destiny is on my side, Bentick! I know that quite certainly, my friend, and destiny has laid down certain laws that must eventually be recognised and given justice by humans. One of those laws is that humans can, to varying degrees, control their own destiny, as well as that of those around them.' He halted in his stride and looked at Bentick again. Then he continued quietly: 'And if a person can foresee something of what's going to happen, they can order the relative context of events to suit their own purpose!'

Bentick felt a prickle of fear at the back of his brain. 'You're clever but mighty dangerous, Professor!' he said sharply. 'I don't think you realise what you're saying. A person has a will of their own, but things beyond that are outside our understanding. I'd advise you to be very careful how you play with your toys, sir!'

The scientist gave an angry snort, but

kept back any reply he might have made to the agent's words. Bentick fingered his chin, watching him narrowly. He felt helpless to stop this man from doing things that he knew instinctively were dangerous. His only hope was that Barringville, when the professor showed him the Telecopter in action, would have the good sense to realise the peril behind it. In the meantime, Bentick was determined to protect himself and others as best he could. Carol was locked in her own room; she ought to be all right. Nargan had already been badly scared by the Telecopter and Dale, and was highly unlikely to venture through the steel door to the laboratory again. There remained Barringville, but he was in no corporeal danger from the scientist; the two were friends of considerable standing. Yet if Dale happened to tune in to some scene of violence from the past or in the future, then even friends might suffer from the dread and intangible emanations of the screen.

Feeling very uncomfortable, Bentick met the eyes of the professor. They were mad eyes, there was little doubt about that. And there was triumph in them now. The triumph of a man who knows in his heart that he has won a major victory over another.

Bentick was on the point of making some soothing remark in an attempt to disengage himself when a sound from the hallway outside attracted his attention. Dale, too, heard the door of the library open and close. There were voices, Nargan's loudest. Barringville spoke in his own quiet, cultured tones. The police officer said something that Bentick did not catch. Then footsteps came across the hall.

Dale leapt towards the partially open door, dragging it inwards and flinging himself through. Bentick gave a shrug. The man was impatient, he thought. He must want to see Barringville pretty badly, yet the two of them had already spent some time talking together before the conference with Nargan. It was all a bit odd. But then there were many things that were odd in this business.

He followed the professor into the hall

more slowly, to find that Nargan was halfway up the stairs while Dale and Barringville were standing facing each other outside the library. Dale had his back to Bentick, and Barringville caught the agent's eye as he came towards them. The statesman was saying: 'Certainly, Dale; I shall be only too delighted. But first of all, let me have a word with Bentick, and I must have some time to go over the results of this talk with Nargan.' He smiled at his friend. 'They're rather important, you know!'

'Of course, my dear fellow!' Dale said. 'Sorry, but I run away with myself.' He turned and saw Bentick. At the same time, the agent chanced to look towards the stairs. Nargan had halted and was standing with one hand on the bannister, his head cocked inquisitively, listening to everything that passed between Dale and Barringville.

The professor did not notice Nargan. He went on: 'There are a few things besides the Telecopter that I feel you must see. Things that will be useful to Britain.'

A frown crossed Barringville's face. 'Be

quiet!' he said quickly. 'Wait until we're alone, Professor. These matters aren't for idle discussion.'

Bentick coughed loudly behind Dale's back. The scientist swung round almost angrily. He, too, caught sight of Nargan on the stairs. The diplomat beamed in an oily fashion and turned away, continuing his way upwards.

Dale sighed as he saw the frown on Barringville's face. 'Well,' he said, 'my offer still stands. You're invited to see the Tele-copter in action, but I do ask you not to keep me waiting longer than you have to. This machine may eventually control our lives more fully than we can ourselves.'

Barringville eyed him shrewdly. 'You know,' he said, 'I'm rather afraid that you may be right, Dale.'

15

The Telecopter Strikes

Dale and Barringville stood quite still for a moment, their eyes locked in a silent battle as if they were measuring each other up. Bentick watched with a queer sense of detachment. This affair had gone out of his reach, he thought. The major issues behind it were now in the hands of these two widely differing personalities. Something of the power each man was capable of struck him, but left him distant, having no part in what was going on.

Dale shrugged. 'We shall see,' was all he said, but there was an omen in the words.

Barringville inclined his head gravely. 'Undoubtedly, my friend,' he replied gently. Then he turned away and exchanged a glance with Bentick. 'I shall be in the library for a time,' he said. 'If you want me for anything, don't hesitate to come in. The professor, I'm sure, is a busy man, and will excuse me while I go over these details.' He patted the thick briefcase under his arm.

Dale gave him a final meaningful look that Bentick could not interpret; then he, too, moved away. Barringville entered the library and closed the door behind him. Bentick was left alone in the empty hall, the policeman having already returned to his companions in one of the cars. Bentick heard the professor go into the kitchen, and a moment later the steel door clanged as it shut.

Bentick frowned, rubbed his chin, and glanced at the stairs speculatively. Carol was up there, he thought. So was Nargan. He was glad that Carol had locked herself in.

He went back into the dining room and stood at the window for a minute, thinking. Was there anything he could usefully do? There didn't seem to be, and that was what niggled at his mind more than all the rest of his troubles put together. He could not prevent Barringville from going down to see the Telecopter, yet he was sure that no good would come of it. And then there was also Nargan to consider. The diplomat had overheard those intriguing remarks made by Dale in the hall. Obviously his curiosity had been aroused by the professor's words, but where that would lead he could not tell.

His thoughts might have drifted on and on in this rather hopeless strain had not Barringville opened the door of the library and called his name. Bentick went across the hall quickly, glad of something to do and hoping to learn some more from the statesman.

Barringville smiled and stood aside. 'Come in,' he said. 'I think you should know that I'll shortly be going down to Dale's laboratory. There seems to be some doubt in your mind as to whether it's a wise move, but in the interests of my duty, I feel bound to go. Dale is a clever man, and there's always a chance that he may have struck upon something that will be invaluable to us. That's the sole reason I want to see this machine he's just invented. Though what use it could be to a country such as ours, I fail to see at the moment.'

'Count me in on that!' said Bentick firmly. 'It's a crazy thing if you ask me, sir. And Dale's crazy, too!'

'I think you're probably right,' agreed Barringville. 'However, I mean to go down to the laboratory. Would you care to come with me?' He watched Bentick closely as he put the question to him.

Bentick hesitated. He did not want to see the Telecopter in action again, yet he could hardly refuse. 'I'll come if you wish me to,' he answered with little enthusiasm. 'But first of all, I'd like to run upstairs and make sure that Miss Collins is all right. I told her to stay in her room till Nargan left. He isn't a pleasant type, as you know, and she's frightened of him.'

'By all means,' said Barringville. 'In the meanwhile, I'll carry on down. I can find my own way.'

Bentick nodded. 'I'll follow in just a minute, sir.'

He waited till Barringville had disappeared from sight, and then made his way thoughtfully to the foot of the stairs. He felt as if he carried a weight on his shoulders, yet could not identify exactly what ingredients comprised it. Maybe Carol; maybe Barringville and Nargan. Maybe just the very existence of Dale's Telecopter with all its odd and sinister implications.

He tried to shrug away the feeling of oppression. Glancing upwards, he was in time to see Nargan appear at the top of the stairway and halt, watching him with a cunning light in his small eyes. Bentick started up the stairs towards him. He presumed the man was coming down. At any rate, he thought with relief, he'd be shot of Nargan before long. That would be one thing less to worry about. A very unpleasant thing, too!

Nargan waited till Bentick reached him on the first landing. The agent met his gaze but said nothing, waiting for the other to make the initial move if there was to be one. The diplomat frowned. 'I shall be in the library for a time,' he announced at length. 'I have some writing to do. After that, I shall probably be ready to leave this place. You'll stay nearby to attend me.'

'Give me a call when you want me,' answered Bentick in a flat, hard tone. 'I'll be delighted to escort you back to the airport.'

Nargan looked at him coldly. He seemed as if he were about to say something more, but changed his mind and merely nodded instead. Bentick watched his broad back as he passed and went on down the stairs. He himself continued to the corridor off which Carol's room opened. With an unconscious quickening of his pulse, he came to a halt outside her door and paused before knocking. Then his knuckles rapped softly on the panel, and he waited.

There was no answer, so he knocked again. Still nothing happened; no sound broke the stillness of the lonely house. A newborn fear gripped Bentick with icy fingers as it dawned on him that Carol was not in the room. He knew she could not be there, or she would have answered his knock in some fashion.

He reached out and grasped the door handle firmly, turning it slowly and carefully. The door opened inwards without noise or effort. He drew a breath and looked inside. The room was empty.

Bentick stood on the threshold for a moment in a rising flood of indecision. What had happened? Where had Carol gone? She had promised not to leave her room, yet something must have happened to take her from it.

His eyes raked everywhere with a sudden keenness, but there was no sign of a scribbled note or anything to indicate when or how she had gone or where she was. His forehead creased with furrows as he glanced out into the corridor again. She must be somewhere around, he thought savagely.

He turned about and searched every room on the upper floor of the long, low house. Even Nargan's came in for a hasty investigation, but again he drew a blank that brought renewed fears to his brain and clouded his powers of reasoning.

Not until he was standing at the top of the stairway, rubbing his chin furiously and wracking his brain for some clue, did it enter his head that the prompting of the Telecopter might have influenced her so strongly that her will had been destroyed and her body had answered that powerful, insidious call. He went over every detail of their last conversation in his mind, trying to pick out the important parts and piece them together. She had been unsure of herself, he remembered. And afraid, too, though she'd hidden it well.

Bentick pulled himself together, grabbing at his frayed nerves in an attempt to see things clearly. If Carol had been overcome by that dangerous prompting, it was useless searching for her anywhere but in Dale's laboratory. And already Barringville was down there with the professor. Perhaps even now the Telecopter was working, revealing to them the strange events of the past and future.

Bentick wasted no more time in speculation. He ran down the stairs two at a time, sprinting across the hall and making for the kitchen. As he entered the big high-roofed room with its old-fashioned fittings and the remains of a hasty breakfast on the table, he heard voices near at hand. Halting just inside the door, he glanced quickly at the laboratory entrance.

Professor Dale was standing in the partially open doorway. Facing him, with his back to Bentick, was Nargan. Dale said: 'But of course, my friend. You are as welcome as anyone to visit my laboratory again. Come along down. Mr. Barringville is there already, and I was about to give him a demonstration of some highly important apparatus. Please join us.' He beamed at Nargan.

Bentick halted and waited, hardly daring to breathe. What, he wondered, had happened to force Nargan to overcome his fear of the Telecopter and seek out the scientist once more in this fashion? It was obvious that the diplomat must have gone to the kitchen almost immediately after leaving Bentick on the upper floor. Was he, perhaps, expecting to learn some secret that would prove of value to himself or the country he represented? Bentick thought it likely. There was no other solution which fitted the facts, for a short time ago he felt sure that nothing would have induced Nargan to visit Dale a second time. Only the man's inherent greed for information might have had the desired effect in steadying his nerves sufficiently to venture into the laboratory.

Nargan did not hesitate in accepting Dale's ready invitation. 'I'll follow you down, Professor,' he said calmly. 'There's no need for you to worry about my feelings in making this visit. I can control them perfectly.'

Bentick waited, still watching Nargan's back as he moved in the wake of Dale. The professor had not noticed the agent in the doorway, being wholly absorbed with Nargan.

The steel door was left ajar as the two disappeared through the opening. Bentick could hear them moving along the corridor till their footsteps faded as they reached the stairs leading down. Not till that happened did the agent attempt to follow. Then he moved swiftly and certainly, eager to reach the laboratory not far behind the others. He wondered if Carol would be down there as he feared, and if the professor would try any more of his tricks to take advantage of her keen sensitivity.

When he reached the gallery he halted, looking down into the brightly lit vault below. He hardly knew what he expected to find when he got there, but in actual fact everything before his eyes was so prosaic and ordinary that he experienced a sense of flatness that startled him.

Barringville and Nargan were standing together with their backs to the scientist's crowded bench. Bentick saw that Nargan's podgy hands were gripped on the edges of the leather-seated cocktail stool he himself had sat on the previous night. Barringville stood without support, one hand in his trouser pocket and the other holding a smoking cigarette as he listened attentively to whatever the professor was saying.

Bentick closed his ears to the words. He knew it was information about the broad principles involved in the working of the Telecopter, for Dale was resting a hand on the machine and emphasising his points with jabs of his other hand.

Bentick went on standing at the junction of the gallery, his eyes raking every corner of the laboratory in search of Carol. There was so much material and apparatus packed on the floor that it was difficult to tell if she was there, but he did not think she could be. None of the three men below had as yet noticed his presence, so he could take his time about going down, and wait for further developments. He decided to wait until Dale put out the lights and turned on the Telecopter, as he felt sure he would. Meanwhile, his eyes continued to hunt for Carol among the scattered blocks of shadow that filled the enormous vault in spite of its generally brilliant lighting.

But look as he would, he failed to see any sign of her. Her disappearance was a mystery that troubled him deeply, but he was glad that as far as he could tell she was not in the laboratory. In this gloomy, sinister place, there was danger for her as well as for the others.

As these and many other thoughts crossed his mind, he became aware that Professor Dale was finishing the initial part of his demonstration and would soon be proving to Barringville that the Telecopter was capable of doing all he claimed. He heard Dale ask Barringville to reach behind him and turn off the main lighting. At the same time, he was aware of the hum of the generator starting up as Dale threw the switches. The laboratory was plunged into almost total darkness as Barringville did as the scientist requested. Then Bentick was once again watching with a fascinated gaze as the opalescent screen of the Telecopter glowed and shimmered with its eerie radiance.

Professor Dale adjusted the controls till pictures from the past were built up and presented by the cosmic radiation and echoes on which it drew. Bentick, who had already seen some of these disjointed fragments from the pages of history, found himself just as enthralled as if he were seeing them for the first time. He saw those conspirators again, huddled in the ancient vault as they plotted and planned their coup. A sudden thought — that the age-old murder would again be re-enacted — troubled Bentick and awoke him from the grip of the emanations of the Telecopter. Taking a firm grasp on his nerves and forcing himself to move quietly and calmly, he started down the steps to the floor of the laboratory. Unconsciously his fingers tightened on the butt of his automatic as he reached the bottom and crept silently up behind Barringville. Keeping one eye on Nargan's dark shape close at hand, he listened as Dale talked clearly. His features were illuminated in the shifting, restless glow of the screen. It was hard to tell what manner of expression he wore; but his voice, though tense, was under control.

'What you'll witness in a moment,' he was saying, 'is a scene that altered history. It's a scene of violence and death, treachery and murder. Hundreds of years ago, the conspiracy you've just seen took place in this crypt. It was followed shortly afterwards by the political murder I shall now endeavour to bring from the mists of the past!'

Bentick, who knew what was coming, braced himself and tried in vain to keep his eyes from the opalescent screen before him. Nargan, too, was afraid of the picture he would see, and Bentick sensed his fear as an unseen influence in the darkness nearby.

Only Barringville appeared to be enjoying himself. He made no murmur of protest as the professor brought the screen to life again and two solitary figures were revealed. Bentick, despite his determination, found himself staring at them fixedly. All the emotions that had once before asserted themselves were there in his mind again. He knew the fear and uncertainty of the young man who would shortly be killed before his eyes. He felt the greed and cunning of the old white-bearded man. And he felt and fought the suddenly overpowering urge to kill as well.

Completely under the spell of the Telecopter, he felt his fingers grip the automatic in his pocket. He was quite oblivious to other people around him in the gloom. He barely heard the drone of Professor Dale's keyed-up voice as the scientist went on explaining how the Telecopter worked. No one was listening, Bentick knew. He had no mind of his own in any event. The gun in his hand came out of his pocket. He could not have held it concealed any longer had he wanted to.

An overwhelming desire to absorb all the emotions of those two ghostly figures on the screen entered his brain. In a moment now, he knew, the old man would strike at the other's back with that glistening blade, and the murder would be done.

He was suddenly aware of Nargan's stifled breathing close beside him in the shadows. Dale was nothing but a figure in the ghostly light alongside the Telecopter. Then to Bentick he swiftly grew to be a target for that dreadful impulse to kill.

The screen flickered madly for an instant. Bentick saw the image of the old man raise his hand, grasping his knife as the young man turned away. In less than a second now . . .

There was a swift, strangled cry from somewhere in the darkness beyond the Telecopter. Bentick gave a start and pulled himself together. The sound of the cry had an electric effect on him. But by then other things were happening, things entirely beyond his control.

Following hard on the heels of the strangled cry came a harsh explosion of sound. Bentick realised too late that a gun had been fired. At the same time he heard a thud and a gasping, choking sob at his side. Professor Dale gave a shout that was a cross between triumph and fear. Then Nargan sagged and slumped to the ground in an untidy sprawl as Barringville turned on the main lights, flooding the laboratory with brilliance that was welcome.

Not until then did Bentick fully realise what had happened. He saw Carol swaying as she crossed the floor towards them. He saw the professor. He saw Nargan, dead at his feet. They were all like unreal beings. Only Barringville was calm and solid. And he suddenly yelled a warning.

'Look out!' he rapped. 'Bentick — look out or there'll be another murder!'

16

Future Turned to Present

Bentick tore his eyes from Nargan's body and his gaze met that of Professor Dale, who had a smoking gun in his right hand. There was madness in the scientist's face and the threat of coming death in the way he crouched at the side of his Telecopter.

Barringville started towards him impulsively. It was then that Bentick acted. He grabbed at Barringville's arm and whirled him aside impatiently. The gun in Dale's hand spat flame once more, but the bullet zipped between Bentick and the statesman. Bentick fired in turn and knocked the gun from the professor's grasp. With the coming of light in the laboratory, the urge to kill was dying within him. He could see clearly now that Dale had done a dreadful thing in shooting Nargan. But he himself had been under the spell of the machine and could have murdered Dale with just as much detachment as Dale had murdered the diplomat. Even in the heat of the moment, Bentick found himself wondering what reaction Barringville had experienced.

'Thank heaven for that!' said the statesman. 'Watch him, Bentick, while I see if Nargan's alive.'

But Dale was not finished yet. As Barringville moved behind Bentick, the professor, letting go of his injured hand, grabbed a slim-bladed screwdriver and rushed forward in a mad, impetuous attack that was blind to danger.

Bentick waited till the last possible moment. Dale reached him and grasped his throat, at the same time making a dangerous stab with his improvised weapon. Bentick hit him in the stomach. He heard Carol scream from not far away. Then the professor, now completely insane, tried to kill him again.

How it happened, Bentick was never entirely sure, but Barringville rushed forward, gripping Dale by the shoulders. Then Bentick's gun went off as Dale struck his hand a paralysing blow. In a moment it was all over.

Bentick staggered clear, standing on the floor of the underground laboratory with a still-smoking gun in his hand. Dale lay dead. Barringville, his face clouded with the deepest worry, stared at Bentick. 'He killed Nargan,' he announced in an unemotional voice. 'What will happen now, I can't bear to think.'

'And I killed Dale,' said Bentick grimly. 'I don't know how, but it's done.'

Barringville shook his head. 'I should never have listened to him. These events must have been on his mind for a long time. I see now that he hated Nargan and meant to destroy him no matter what the consequences.'

Bentick was hardly listening to what the statesman was saying. His eyes had sought out and met those of Carol. She stood to one side, one hand to her mouth as if to stifle a cry that would not come. She was shaking in every limb.

Bentick went towards her. He felt tenderness welling up within him. She swayed and almost fell, her eyes dilated as they stared at the body of Dale. Nargran did not matter to her, but with the professor it was a different thing. Despite her inherent fear of him, and her knowledge that he had always been a little unbalanced, she was still under the spell of her loyalty towards him. Now the scientist was dead, and she had seen him die with her own eyes.

Suddenly Bentick was beside her, putting his arm round her shoulder protectively and driving away all the terror from her being. Without a word she turned to him, burying her face against his coat and quivering as he held her closely. He glanced up and met Barringville's eyes across the body of Dale.

'You'd better take her upstairs out of this,' said Barringville. 'Send a couple of men down, will you? I'll wait here till they come. I've got to have time to think, Bentick. This is a frightful business, but there may be some way through.'

Bentick only nodded slightly. Then he lifted Carol in his arms and carried her to the foot of the steps leading up to the gallery. As he went he remembered all that had happened, and how the Telecopter had foretold the grim events of the past few minutes. He recalled how he was even now carrying Carol in his arms. How he had stood with a smoking gun in his hand. Why had he not seen more? If he had, he might have been in a position to prevent Nargan's death as well as Dale's. But he realised that if he had seen the deaths on the Telecopter screen, they would have happened with the same inevitability as all the smaller, less important details that had occurred.

Bentick took Carol straight to her room and set her on the bed. She was silent and dry-eyed now, but shaken by some inner emotion that could find no escape for the moment. That, thought Bentick with relief, would come later on.

Neither of them spoke a word. Bentick stayed by the bed looking down at her, his face revealing the mingled feelings that wracked him. Then he turned away and went from where Carol lay, with one arm across her forehead. The very faintest of smiles suddenly crinkled the corners of her mouth. Bentick opened the door and went outside, closing it softly behind him.

His mind was seething with a dozen

different thoughts. There was the death of Nargan to cope with and the disastrous effects it might have; and the death of Professor Dale as well. That was another awkward thing to handle. What would happen to the Telecopter now that its inventor was dead? Would Barringville have any notions on that score? Bentick could not imagine that the Telecopter would prove of much material use to the country. Its evil influence had already caused the death of two men, and it could well cause more, unless someone smashed it up and destroyed Dale's blueprints. Bentick had half a mind to do the smashing himself.

In the hall downstairs, he located the police officer who had been standing guard during Barringville and Nargan's conference. Not having heard the shots, the officer looked at Bentick's grim face in astonishment A few brief words sent the man running outside the house to fetch one of his companions. Together they accompanied Bentick through the kitchen and into the laboratory.

Barringville was still standing moodily,

looking down at the two dead men. At the sounds of their approach, he raised his head sharply as if shaking himself to wakefulness. 'Glad you got back, Bentick,' he said calmly. 'This is bad. In fact, I fail to see how it could be worse, but I'm hoping that everything will play out rather less tragically than I feared at first.' His words sounded almost stilted to Bentick, who glanced at him keenly. But the statesman was giving nothing away.

Barringville spoke to the police officers, handing over the disposal of the bodies to them; then he and Bentick started up the steps side by side. Both were silent till they reached the kitchen and walked to the library. Then Barringville gestured to a chair, and Bentick sat down with a feeling of acute uneasiness. The statesman stood with his back towards him, staring through the windows at the rolling moorland outside and the long, twisting, overgrown driveway that led to the house.

His first words gave Bentick something of a shock. 'If I'd had a weapon, I'd have killed someone down there myself,' said Barringville in a flat tone of voice. 'It was as much as I could do to keep any control of myself at all. Only that woman screaming suddenly broke the spell. I can understand how Dale came to murder Nargan. It was the influence of the Telecopter, of course. I wish now I'd taken more notice of your warning, Bentick. What will happen I hate to think, but you need attach no blame to yourself. All the responsibility rests on me.' He turned and met Bentick's steady gaze.

'Thank you, sir,' said Bentick. 'But after all, it was my job to guard Nargan. And I failed in that, no two ways about it.' He pulled a rueful face. 'My chief won't be as generous as you are; but that's not the point.'

Barringville eyed him steadily. Then he nodded his head in a slow, judicial fashion. 'I'll have a word with Cain myself,' he said quietly. 'In the meantime, you'd better make your report in the usual manner. Use the dining room; I shall need this room and the telephone for a while myself.' He hesitated. Then: 'How's the woman?' he asked, watching Bentick closely.

'She was all right when I left her.'

'Make sure she's still all right, then. Convey my sympathy to her, will you? It must be a shock for her to realise that her guardian is dead, though I feel that living here with Dale must've been a strain on someone so young.'

Bentick contented himself with a murmured word of thanks, then he left the room and paused in the hall. The house was very quiet; it might have been a tomb. He made for the stairs, but before he reached them a telephone started shrilling stridently. Bentick hesitated. The phone stopped ringing as Barringville lifted the receiver in the library. Bentick went on upstairs without interrupting.

He tapped on Carol's door and waited. Her answer came in a hushed voice from within. Bentick opened the door and smiled when he saw she was looking better than the last time he saw her. There was a trace of colour in her cheeks now, and she actually raised a smile in return as he stood in the open doorway.

Bentick was on the point of speaking to her when there was a call from the lower floor of the house. He recognised

Barringville's voice and turned with a frown. The statesman sounded oddly excited. Bentick made a hasty excuse to Carol and left her.

'Come here,' said Barringville when Bentick reached the hall. 'I've good news — for both of us!'

Bentick followed him to the library, wondering what in the world could have happened to change the statesman so quickly from worry to excitement.

Barringville started without preamble. 'I've just had a call from London.' His eyes were gleaming. 'The man who died in the laboratory was *not* Nargan! He was an impostor. A spy! A clever one, I admit, for he fooled us all; but luckily he didn't get away with anything.'

Bentick gaped in amazement. 'But his credentials were all in order,' he said, mystified. 'I'd never have brought him here if they hadn't been. And he fitted the description I was given. I don't understand!'

'He would!' said Barringville dryly. 'He apparently followed the real Nargan, held him up, and locked him in an empty room across the Channel, then assumed his disguise. Through a security leak, he already knew the passwords and all the rest of it. He was sent, of course, on behalf of one of our most bitter enemies, but thanks to the Telecopter he failed to return with the information they sought. The real Nargan was discovered last night, but word has only just reached us of what happened.'

Bentick whistled softly. 'Then there's been no damage done, sir? What a relief!' He paused. 'Maybe Professor Dale's instinctive dislike of him wasn't such a bad thing after all.'

'Not a word of this to anyone but those directly concerned,' Barringville said with a nod. 'Another meeting has already been arranged between Nargan and myself, but I doubt if you'll be in on that. Cain has other work more agreeable to your taste.' He smiled at the agent.

'May I tell Carol — Miss Collins, sir?'

Barringville said he could, but he was relying on their common sense not to spread the news further.

Bentick went up the stairs two at a

time. He wasted little time in passing on the stupendous news to Carol, and her relief when she heard it knew no bounds.

'Poor Professor Dale,' she said presently. 'I almost wish I hadn't been so afraid of him and the Telecopter. He must've known there was something wrong with Nargan — or, I should say, the man we thought was Nargan.'

Bentick smiled down at her upturned face. 'Perhaps he did,' he answered slowly. 'Perhaps he knew a whole lot more than we thought. Remember, he brought a lot of the future into the present time. For myself, I'm content to live in the present.'

She was watching him with a peculiar light in her eyes. 'So am I,' she whispered. 'The future is always in front of us, but I'm not afraid of it any longer.'

'Nor am I,' answered Bentick. 'Not anymore. You see, Carol, I can foresee everything I want to about the future without having to use a machine like the Telecopter.'

She made no reply. She had no need to. It was all there for Bentick to read in her face.

BLACK BARGAIN

Victor Rousseau

Joan Wentworth, a newly qualified nurse, nearly faints from the ether whilst assisting the famous surgeon, Dr. Lancaster, and is promptly suspended from her job. That evening, when she pleads with him to reinstate her, she is surprised to be invited to work at his hospice that serves the poor hill people of Pennsylvania. Joan accepts; but on her arrival at the remote institute, she finds herself plunged into an atmosphere of menace and mystery. No one there seems to be normal — not least Dr. Lancaster himself when he visits . . .

THE MYSTERY OF BLOODSTONE

V. J. Banis

Ancient Bloodstone Manor stands on a rocky knoll overlooking the village of Skull Point. What is the secret that sends Vanessa and her aged guardian, Tutrice, rushing there despite the violent raging of a storm? What keeps Vanessa's parents prisoner within its walls? Who is the mysterious sailor found half-drowned on the beach, wearing a bloodstone ring that Vanessa recognizes at once? Bloodstone — a house of secrets. A house of mystery. Mysteries that Vanessa must solve if she is ever to know happiness.

BLUE PERIL

Denis Hughes

Complicit in Doctor Brooking's efforts to create a monster, Gregory Conrad is ultimately forced to make the main contribution himself, losing his life in the process. However, Brooking discovers that the thing his genius has brought to life possesses a will of its own, as well as superhuman powers . . . Jerry Tern, an investigative reporter, and Vivienne Conrad, Gregory's sister, join forces to investigate her brother's disappearance, but soon become captives of the monster — the so-called Blue Peril of the popular press — and witness at first hand its reign of terror . . .

THE SECRET OF BENJAMIN SQUARE

Michael Kurland

When a stranger calls at their New England farmhouse to inform Nancy and her brother Robert that they are the heirs of a British nobleman, and that a fortune can be theirs if they agree to move to the ancestral home of Benjamin House in London, it seems like all their childhood dreams have come true. But upon arrival, Nancy is soon homesick — while Robert nearly loses his life in an 'accident'. Then there's the mysterious ancient riddle connected with the house that could point the way to hidden treasure . . .

COME AND BE KILLED

Shelley Smith

Prescribed a holiday out of London to recover from nervous exhaustion, Florence Brown is betrayed and furious when her sister refuses to accompany her. A unsuccessful attempt to take her own life sees her dispatched to a grim nursing-home. Mid-way through her escape from the place, she encounters the genial Mrs. Jolly, who invites Florence to stay with her as a paying guest. But her new friend is not all she seems, and Florence is in deadly danger . . .